EKK

Presented by the

Friends of the

Northampton Free Library

Book Endowment Fund

RESCUED

ALSO BY DAVID ROSENFELT

RESCUED

David Rosenfelt

MINOTAUR BOOKS
NEW YORK

This is a work of fiction. All of the characters, organizations, and events portrayed in this novel are either products of the author's imagination or are used fictitiously.

RESCUED. Copyright © 2018 by Tara Productions, Inc. All rights reserved. Printed in the United States of America. For information, address St. Martin's Press, 175 Fifth Avenue, New York, N.Y. 10010.

www.minotaurbooks.com

Library of Congress Cataloging-in-Publication Data

Names: Rosenfelt, David, author.
Title: Rescued / David Rosenfelt.
Description: First edition. | New York : Minotaur Books, 2018. | Series: An Andy
    Carpenter mystery
Identifiers: LCCN 2018012217 | ISBN 9781250133069 (hardcover) | ISBN 9781250199577
    (signed edition) | ISBN 9781250133083 (ebook)
Subjects: LCSH: Carpenter, Andy (Fictitious character)—Fiction. | Agency (Law)—
    New Jersey—Fiction. | Murder—Investigation—Fiction. | Animal shelters—Fiction. |
    Dog rescue—Fiction. | GSAFD: Suspense fiction. | Mystery fiction.
Classification: LCC PS3618.O838 R43 2018 | DDC 813'.6—dc23
LC record available at https://lccn.loc.gov/2018012217

Our books may be purchased in bulk for promotional, educational, or business use. Please contact your local bookseller or the Macmillan Corporate and Premium Sales Department at 1-800-221-7945, extension 5442, or by email at MacmillanSpecialMarkets@macmillan.com.

10 9 8 7 6 5 4

RESCUED

It wasn't the presence of the tractor trailer that caused John Paxos to take notice.

He was in a rest area off the Garden State Parkway near Paterson, New Jersey, and he figured that truck drivers needed to rest and use the bathroom like anyone else. There were truck stops nearby, but maybe this guy just couldn't wait.

The weird way it was parked, at an angle, struck Paxos as strange, but maybe the guy had to go really bad. There was no particular reason for him to park carefully; there was plenty of room. In fact, there were no other cars until Paxos arrived.

But a couple of other factors bothered him. When Paxos used the restroom, he didn't see anyone else in there. Maybe the driver was female? When he came out, he could hear that the engine in the truck was still running. That made no sense at all; he could just drive off with the truck if he wanted to. Fortunately for the careless driver, Paxos was a pharmacist, not a thief. And his passion was collecting vintage cars; the tractor trailer didn't quite fit the collection.

There was certainly the chance that the driver was in the back of the truck, maybe readjusting whatever it was he was hauling. Of course, that was it. Paxos was about to accept that and walk away, get back on the road, but something stopped him from doing so.

It was just a feeling, but it was a feeling that made him call out "Hello?" a few times, each time a bit louder than the time before it. But there was no response from the driver.

And that's when he heard the barking.

It wasn't just one dog; that much was certain. It seemed like there must have been an army of dogs in that truck; Paxos would later estimate the number at thirty and would be very low at that. What kind of a tractor trailer hauled dogs as cargo?

So he called out again, though against the sound of the barking, there was no way anyone could have heard him. But if the dogs had heard his earlier call, and the fact that it started the barking indicated they had, then a person in the truck should have heard it as well. Yet no one had responded.

Paxos couldn't just leave the rest stop, not with the dogs on the truck. It could be hot back there; at the very least he knew he had to call someone. Maybe local animal control or the police.

He decided on animal control, so he got them on the phone and told them what he knew, which wasn't much. He promised to wait for them; they said it would take ten minutes to get there.

But Paxos didn't want to tell them when they arrived that he hadn't even checked out the dogs on the truck, and he wanted to know what he was dealing with. So after a few minutes of thinking about it, he cautiously stepped up on to the truck and looked toward the sound of the barking.

And that's when he saw the blood.

Andy, it's Ralph."

Caller ID had said "Private Caller," and I don't recognize the voice on the line. The only "Ralph" that comes to mind is Kramden, but I doubt that's who's calling me.

"Did you say Ralph?" I ask.

"Ralph . . . Brandenberger. Andy, you have to get over here."

That clears it up. Ralph Brandenberger is the director of the Passaic County Animal Shelter. My friend Willie Miller and I run the Tara Foundation, a dog rescue organization named after my golden retriever, who is the greatest dog in the history of the universe. We often help Ralph out when his shelter is overcrowded by taking dogs and finding homes for them.

I don't know that I've ever talked to Ralph on the phone, which might be why his voice seems unfamiliar. But it's more than that; he sounds out of breath, and maybe even scared.

"You want me to come down to the shelter?" I ask.

"No, I'm at the rest stop on the Garden State, near Exit 156. Andy, it's awful . . . please hurry."

"What's wrong?"

I hear some people talking in the background, and Ralph says, "I can't talk now. They're telling me to move back. Please, Andy."

Click.

I'm left with a sense of dread. If Ralph is calling me and needs my help about something "awful," it must involve dogs being hurt, or injured, or abused. And if there is anything I hate in this world, it's animals being hurt, or injured, or abused.

My wife, Laurie, is out shopping with our son, Ricky, so I can't ask her to go with me. Instead I call Willie Miller, which comes with its own level of risk. Willie can be volatile, and when that volatility is combined with his expertise in karate, he can be extremely dangerous.

If there is a human identified with abusing a dog, and if Willie is within proximity of that human, it can get very ugly, very quickly. Willie is a bigger dog lunatic than I am, and that is saying something.

But I call him, and I tell him I'll pick him up at the foundation, since it's on the way. He's waiting outside when I pull up, and he spends the next ten minutes asking me questions that I can't answer. I look over and see that his fist is clenched into a ball; I'm sure he's painted a mental picture of a scene that includes an abused animal and an abuser that is within his reach.

"Take it easy, Willie," I say, a suggestion that has zero chance of having any impact whatsoever.

"I got this one," he says.

I don't know what he means by that, but I don't have time to ponder it. We get to the rest stop but can't pull in, because the entrance is blocked by police tape. The police tape, as it usually is, is guarded by police officers.

We park along the road and walk toward the tape, and an officer I don't recognize says, "You can't come in here."

"My name is Andy Carpenter. This is Willie Miller."

"That supposed to mean something?" He doesn't seem to be aware of my fame; from now on, I probably should carry my press clippings with me.

I see Ralph about twenty yards behind him; he has spotted us and is running toward us. "It's okay," he says to the officer. "They're with me."

The officer is less than impressed by this declaration. "Who the hell are you?"

"I'm the one who called you guys here."

It's a fascinating conversation, but my attention is drawn to another police officer I see. It's Pete Stanton, my closest and only friend in the Paterson Police Department.

Pete is a captain in charge of the homicide division, which makes this situation a whole lot more confusing and ominous. The homicides he investigates are of the human variety, so any incident that involves both Ralph and Pete indicates a puzzling mixture of species.

Pete seems to moan when he sees me; the fact that we are close friends does not insulate me from his disdain for defense attorneys. But he walks over to us and tells the officer that he will handle the situation.

"You here for the dogs, or looking to drum up another client?"

"I have no idea why I'm here. Ralph called me."

Ralph nods. "About the dogs."

"What's going on?"

"We have a truckload of dogs and a murder victim," Pete says.

"Who's the victim?" I ask.

He frowns. "You worry about the dogs." Then he turns to the officer guarding the perimeter and says, "You can let them in. If he starts to act like a defense attorney, you have my permission to shoot him."

Pete walks back to what must be the murder scene, leaving Ralph, Willie, and me alone.

"What's the situation?" I say.

"Andy, you're not going to believe it."

There are sixty-one dogs in the truck," Ralph says. "According to the records, the guy was bringing them up from down South. You know, to be rescued."

I do know what he's talking about. The unwanted animal situation in the Northeast is light-years better than down South, and hundreds of dogs are taken out of the great danger of euthanasia and brought up here every year. Most of the dogs are taken to New England; I don't yet know the destination of this truck.

"What kind of dogs?"

"All kinds. I didn't get much of a chance to look. The guy who called me told me there was a body, but as soon as I saw it, I ran out of the truck. Dead bodies give me the creeps. But I definitely saw a few seniors, and a golden retriever mother with a bunch of puppies."

"Let's get them off of there," Willie says in his first verbal contribution to the situation.

Ralph shakes his head. "They said we can't. Something about evidence."

"Bullshit," Willie says. "Those dogs are coming off that truck."

"Let me talk to Pete," I say and head over to where he is standing.

Pete is talking to a couple of detectives, both of whom I have previously successfully attacked in cross-examination on the witness stand. So the greeting I get from the group does not feel warm and welcoming.

"Now what?" Pete says, sneering. He doesn't want to show his subordinates that he has anything less than total disdain for this annoying and intruding defense attorney. Showing hatred for me goes a long way toward earning respect in the department.

"Can we take the dogs off the truck?"

"Not yet. We have to process them and check for evidence."

"You going to interrogate each one?" I ask. "Maybe hook them up to a lie detector? I hear there's a lab mix that looks a little shady; you might be able to get a confession out of him."

He points out to me that they are looking for any possible trace evidence but certainly don't expect to find any. He estimates that it will take a few hours.

"A few hours? You might want to walk them, or it might get a little unpleasant in there. And they might just piss all over your trace evidence."

He hadn't thought of that, and the prospect causes him to revise his estimate to about an hour.

I drive Willie and Ralph over to a rental car place about five minutes away, and Willie's wife, Sondra, meets us there. We rent three large vans that we can use to transport the dogs once they are released by the police.

Sondra calls a bunch of people who occasionally volunteer for our foundation. Their activities generally consist simply of walking, petting, and loving the dogs, all of which is much appreciated. Sondra reports that they will meet us at the foundation when we arrive.

Pete's estimate of one hour proves to be twenty minutes off, and the dogs are getting pretty uncomfortable by the time we get them off the truck. We give each of them a quick walk before loading them into the vans, a process which takes another hour. All of this has to be stressful for them, but they're handling it well.

The dogs are in all shapes, sizes, and ages. The golden retriever looks positively grateful when we take her puppies from her; they've obviously been driving her crazy. Little does she know that she'll be reunited with them very soon.

Sondra has gone back to the foundation building, and she and the volunteers are waiting for us when Ralph, Willie, and I arrive in the vans with the dogs.

Sondra is an unbelievable organizer and planner; if she had been in charge of D-day, by sundown the Allies would have been slurping snow cones on the beach. In record time, all sixty-one dogs are walked, fed, and comfortably placed on beds in their runs.

The foundation is in a building that used to be an ice-skating rink, so we have a lot of space. We wanted it that way, thinking that one day there might be some earthquake, flood, or other disaster that could result in a lot of pets becoming homeless. A shooting at a highway rest stop was not one of the potential disasters that we'd envisioned.

Willie and Sondra will stay at the foundation tonight in case the new dogs need tending to; we have a bedroom set up for them. Our vet will be in tomorrow morning to examine the newcomers, and we'll meet to plan our next steps.

I've called Laurie a few times to update her on what is going on, and now I call to tell her I'll be on the way home. "I'm just going to stop at the market to pick up a couple of things."

"Don't," she says. "Please come straight home."

It's a strange thing to say, made stranger by the tone in which she says it. "Why? What's going on?"

"Just come home, Andy. There's someone here I want you to talk to."

"Who?"

"Can't discuss it now. Just come straight home, please."

I cannot imagine who could be there or what this could be about. That doesn't stop me from attempting to imagine those things all the way home, an effort which proves futile. The odds of Laurie not being able to talk about something and having it be a good thing are pretty small, so at this point what I'm hoping for is the avoidance of a disaster. And whatever bad thing it is, I hope it doesn't involve Ricky.

There's a car in our driveway that I don't recognize; my keen deductive skills tell me it belongs to the person Laurie couldn't talk in front of. There are no revealing bumper stickers on it that might tell me the type of person it is or the identity of the owner, so if I want to find out, I can either break into the car and glove compartment or just walk into the house. It's a tough call, because I don't like breaking into cars, but I have a vague dread of walking into that house.

But at the end of the day, I am Andy Carpenter, courageous to the end, so I walk in.

Laurie is coming out of the den to meet me in the front hallway as I enter.

"What's going on?" I ask. "Who's here?"

"Dave Kramer."

I should have broken into the car.

Dave Kramer is Laurie's ex-boyfriend.

That in itself would make him my hated nemesis.

But it's worse than that.

It was a serious relationship; it lasted almost two years.

But it's worse than that.

He broke up with her.

Besides the obvious fact that breaking up with Laurie makes him the single dumbest human being on the face of the earth, so dumb that he should be watered twice a day, I don't have much more information about him. I know he was once a cop and then a private investigator, and I know Laurie also briefly worked for him after she left the police force.

But that's where my knowledge ends, because Laurie has refused to answer my questions about him. It's possible she took that position because those questions were usually accompanied by my whimpering and moaning, or maybe because they were intrusive and obnoxious. But either way, I soon learned that Dave Kramer was always going to live almost exclusively in my imagination.

Apparently until today.

"Dave Kramer?" I ask, possibly hoping that I misheard her. Maybe she said another name that rhymes with Dave Kramer, like Brave Flamer or Knave Shamer. Maybe I should go break into the car to check.

She nods. "Dave Kramer."

"Are you leaving me?"

"Andy . . . ," she says, frustration in her voice.

"Are you?"

"We're married," she says. "I'd have to get a lawyer, and—"

I interrupt. "I won't represent you in the divorce. And I'll use all my legal brilliance to leave you broken and penniless. You'll be ostracized and humiliated; telemarketers won't take your calls."

"Andy . . ." This time the frustration is mixed with annoyance. "Come in and talk to him."

"Just tell me why he came to see you."

"He didn't. He came to see you."

This comes as a big surprise, but not big enough to shake me into maturity. "Is he going to ask me for your hand?"

This time she doesn't even bother to answer; she just turns and walks back into the kitchen. I know I'm supposed to follow her, but I don't want to. Unfortunately, running away is really not an option, because I live here. And if I hide under the couch, she'll find me.

So I go in and there he is, sitting at my kitchen table, drinking my coffee, and petting my Tara. Tara's got a smile on her face, totally unconcerned that she is showing herself to be a traitor. This, Tara, is the unkindest cut of all.

Our basset hound, Sebastian, sits at the enemy's feet, waiting his turn. I see betrayal everywhere I look.

"Andy, this is Dave Kramer. Dave, Andy."

He gets up to shake my hand, and by that, I mean he really gets up. He's got to be six four; he sort of unfolds as he stands. Since I'm five eleven when wearing two pairs of thick socks, I have to reach up to execute the shake. I hate shaking hands uphill.

I don't usually form opinions about men's looks, but I'm forced to admit that Kramer is good-looking by conventional standards. Of course, I've never been a fan of conventional standards. My own looks are quirky good, and quirky good is the standard I've always adhered to.

"What's going on?" I ask, an open-ended question designed to get this to go wherever it's going in a hurry.

"Laurie and I have been catching up," he says.

"Isn't that nice," I say, which draws a silent, facial reproach from Laurie. I don't know how she does it, but her silent reproaches can be deafening.

"But I came to talk to you," Kramer says. "I'm afraid I might be using my friendship with Laurie to further that end."

I don't respond, because I have nothing to say; he's going to get to wherever this is going, and there's no sense slowing him down.

"I want to hire you as my attorney."

"I'm retired."

"Laurie says you've unsuccessfully retired at least six times."

"This is lucky seven." Then, "Why do you need representation?"

"There was a killing today. A man driving a truckful of dogs was shot and killed inside that truck at a rest stop on the Garden State Parkway. But Laurie tells me you know about it already."

I nod. "I spent the last four hours there, at the scene."

"The police either think I killed the guy, or if they don't yet, they're going to. They will then arrest me."

"Why would they think that?" I ask.

"Because I killed him."

His name is Kenny Zimmer, and he is, or was, a piece of shit. I killed him in self-defense, but he and I have a bit of a history."

"What kind of history?" Laurie asks. I think she can tell I don't want to be involved in this, so apparently her plan is to ask the questions I would ordinarily ask.

"He's the reason I lost my license."

"I didn't realize you did," she says.

He nods. "A business client of mine came to me one day and said his fifteen-year-old daughter had been grabbed and assaulted by a guy in the park. The guy got away, and she went to the police, but they had nothing to go on and didn't even have proof of a crime."

"So the client wanted you to find the perpetrator?"

"Right. Which I did. It was the aforementioned piece of shit, Kenny Zimmer. I so informed the authorities, who weren't inclined to make an arrest."

"Why?"

"I used some unconventional means to break the case. In their defense, nothing that I had would have been admissible. So I don't think they doubted that Zimmer was the guilty party, but they realized they couldn't nail him on it. From their vantage point, it was probably the right call."

"So what did you do?" Laurie asks.

"I went to see Kenny. We discussed the situation at some length, and he admitted his guilt. He actually laughed when he said it. It was one of those annoying little laughs."

"And then?" Laurie prompts.

"I performed some actions that caused him to stop laughing. He went to the cops and filed an assault complaint. Actually, he didn't go to the cops; he called them from the hospital. That was his home for the next three weeks."

"Which is how you lost your license?"

Kramer nods. "I copped to a lesser charge and avoided jail time, but the license was gone."

"You put him in the hospital and you basically got off? How?"

"I had a good reputation with law enforcement, and Kenny didn't. They were glad I did what I did but couldn't openly say so. The courts couldn't punish him, so I had to. Think of it as a glitch in the system."

"How long ago did all this happen? And how have you continued to be an investigator?" Laurie asks.

"It happened about two years ago. Losing the license hasn't changed much; I'm just doing it without official government approval. I lost some of my higher-end clients, but business is still good."

Laurie turns to me. "Andy, you have any questions?"

I shake my head. "Not so far. You're doing fine."

Laurie's got to be frustrated by my attitude, but I'm not feeling pleased about being drawn into this. There are other lawyers, albeit not as brilliant, that he could hire.

"So what happened today?" Laurie asks.

I interrupt. "I don't have a question, but I do have some advice to offer. Be careful what you say here; none of this is privileged."

"Lawyer-client?" he asks.

"I haven't agreed to represent you, and in any event, you haven't hired me yet."

"I'm hoping you will," he says. "But no need to worry, because I'm not going to say anything incriminating. I haven't done anything wrong."

"You've already admitted to assault and a killing," I point out.

"The assault is part of the public record, and the killing was in self-defense."

I nod, accepting his point. "The victim . . . Zimmer. He rescued dogs?"

I think I see a brief smile on Laurie's face; the first one since I got home. She knows that I would be disinclined to be on the side of someone who hurt, never mind killed, a dog rescuer.

Kramer shakes his head. "No, he was a truck driver. He was just paid to drive down South and pick up a bunch of dogs. It was a truck-driving gig; he might as well have been transporting watermelons."

"So how did you come to be on his truck?" Laurie asks, even though being on his truck isn't really the issue. Killing him is a bit more problematic, but I assume eventually we will get around to that.

"It's a long story," he says, "and I don't think we have the time."

As if on cue, the doorbell rings. "See what I mean? That will be the police."

"How did they know you were here?" I ask.

"I told my wife to tell them when they showed up at our house."

"You've got a wife?"

He nods. "Married two years ago. Does that matter?"

"Not a bit," I lie. "Not a bit."

Pete Stanton and three other officers are at the door when I answer it. They have their guns drawn, a prudent move considering that they are here to arrest a murder suspect. For all they know, we could be hostages or in danger. But that doesn't mean I can't mock him for it.

"I hope your bullet is in your shirt pocket, Barney," I say.

It's strange, but he doesn't find that amusing. "Is Kramer in there?"

"He is."

"So you were just down there for the dogs? You forgot to mention that the killer was your client?"

"Once again, you have no idea what you are talking about."

"Bring him out," he says.

"So you can arrest him?"

"No, we just want to share some recipes."

Before I can banter back, Laurie and Kramer come to the door.

"David Kramer?" Pete asks.

"You know who I am, Pete."

Pete tells him that he's under arrest, and one of the other officers reads him his rights. When that's over, Pete says, "Let's go."

I'm sure Kramer must be savvy in this area, but I still tell him, "Don't say anything to anyone. Not a word."

"Are you my lawyer?"

"I'll get back to you on that."

"I hope sooner rather than later."

I nod at his reasonable request. "Definitely sooner."

19

Once they're gone, Laurie turns to me and says, "Where do you want to do this?"

"In bed would be my first choice."

"Andy . . ."

"Kitchen is fine."

We head back to the kitchen to have "the talk." I dread talks that are planned in advance; I can't ever remember a good one. Talks should be spontaneous, not premeditated.

Laurie walks on ahead, and Tara tags along beside me. I say to her, "You and I will talk later, you traitor," but she doesn't seem worried. Sebastian, for his part, doesn't appear to think that observing my talk with Laurie is worth getting up from his dog bed and trudging into the kitchen. He probably knows how it's going to end.

Once we're in the kitchen, Laurie pours us both coffee. "Where should we start?" she says.

"We could flip a coin, but even if I win, I'll just defer to the second half." It's a football reference, and I'm not sure if she got it. What I am sure of is that she ignores it.

"I know Dave Kramer well, Andy. I know him very well."

I don't say anything; I'm just relieved she didn't use the word *carnally*.

She continues. "If he says the killing was in self-defense, it was in self-defense. He is not a liar, and he is not a murderer."

"I believe you. But there are plenty of non-liars and non-murderers that I don't represent."

"And there are plenty that you have."

"True," I say, trying to be as noncommittal as possible. Unfortunately, one of the problems with planned talks is that participants in them eventually have to be committal. It's part of the deal. I just want to put it off as long as possible, but unfortunately, these things have no time limit. I can't run out the clock.

"Would you consider representing him?" she asks.

She could have just asked if I'd represent him, but by adding the word *consider*, it seems like she's willing to take incremental victories. Laurie is a master tactician; it's clear that I am in over my head here.

"I've told you I want to try to cut back on my caseload," I say.

"Cut back? You haven't taken on a case in six months."

"See? It's working," I say. The truth is that I'm independently wealthy from inheritance, previous lucrative cases, and good investments. So I don't need to work, and I don't like to work, which should mean I don't work. Unfortunately, it never seems to pan out that way, the last six glorious months notwithstanding.

"This is the kind of case you have always taken on, someone wrongly accused of murder, whose very life and freedom are at stake."

"I'm already pretty busy," I say. "Ricky starts school in three weeks, and then there's football season, and I need to get the car serviced, and before you know it, it's Halloween. We don't even have costumes yet, and I was hoping not to dress up as a lawyer again this year."

"Andy, are you going to represent him or not?"

"Is it important to you?" There it is, the key question, the absolute decider. Growing up in my house, we could always say no to anything, but when the other family member invoked that personal "importance," it became an imperative. It wasn't used often or casually.

Laurie has accepted this approach, and I can never remember either of us refusing something that the other person said was important. Which means I have officially thrown down the gauntlet; now it's up to Laurie if she wants to pick it up. I'm hoping she won't but betting she will.

"It's important to me that Dave get the best defense possible, and unfortunately that means you," she says.

"So that's a yes? It is important to you?" I ask. I'm looking for some clarity here.

She hesitates a moment before dropping the bomb. "I think so, yes. It is important to me." Then she gives me an out. "But so is your happiness, and I know how much work a case like this can entail."

She has just pulled off a brilliant conversational maneuver; if manipulative negotiating were an Olympic sport, even the Russian judge would give her a ten.

So in case you're scoring at home, here's where things stand: If I refuse her, I will be miserable about it, and so will she. If I give in, I will be miserable, and she'll be happy, albeit a little guilty.

So once again, a planned talk does not go as planned.

"I'll do it."

I take Tara and Sebastian for a walk and then head down to the county jail. If I'm going to be Kramer's lawyer, he has a right to know it without delay. Hopefully he's either hired another lawyer already or confessed.

He's still being processed when I arrive, and I have to wait more than an hour to see him. When I finally do, he asks, "Good news?"

"Depends on your perspective," I say. "If you want to hire me as your lawyer, I'm willing to take the case."

He nods. "You're hired."

"You don't seem surprised at my decision."

"I'm not. I know how persuasive Laurie can be."

"Why me?" I ask.

"She says you're the best."

Some things cannot be argued with, so I don't even try. I tell Kramer that I will be back early in the morning to discuss the case with him, and we can begin to plan our defense. I again admonish him not to talk to anyone about anything, and he assures me that he knows the drill.

Before I leave, I ask, "Is there any message you want me to get to your wife?"

"Oh, about that . . . there is no wife," he says. "I'm not married."

"I don't understand."

"Laurie told me you might be a little weird about she and I having been together, so I figured if you thought I was married, you'd be more inclined to take the case."

"So you lied," I point out.

He nods. "For the greater good. And it seems to have worked."

"Seems to. Let me explain something, also for the greater good. I'm your lawyer; if you lie to me again, about anything, I will instantly not be your lawyer anymore."

"Fair enough," he says.

"Did Laurie know the truth?"

"You'd have to ask her that."

I'm not sure where to go with this. I'm pissed that he lied, and certainly not pleased that he's not actually married. But unfortunately, it all comes back to this being important to Laurie, so it doesn't really change anything. I'm stuck. "See you tomorrow," I say.

It's past seven o'clock when I leave the jail, and as much as I'd like to go home and hide under the bed, I decide to stop at Charlie's. Charlie's is to sports bars what Tara is to living creatures, meaning the absolute best in class.

Before I married Laurie and we adopted Ricky, I used to spend at least three nights a week at Charlie's with Pete Stanton and Vince Sanders, the editor of our local newspaper. Now I'm down to one or two nights, but I can be sure that whenever I do show up, they will be at our regular table, watching sports, drinking beer, and eating burgers and fries.

In my capacity as the only rich person in the group, I wind up getting the check whenever I'm here, and I run a tab, which I pay once a month. Because of that fact, their inherent cheapness always caused them to be glad to see me when I arrived. That changed when I started to notice that they were charging their drinks and meals to my tab even when it was just the two of them.

I haven't mentioned my discovery to them; the truth is that I don't mind paying. A couple of weeks ago, I made an offhand comment that "this place is getting pricey; my tab has been pretty big each month."

I saw them exchange quick glances with each other, and Pete said, "Damn inflation." Vince nodded and said, "It's those bastards in Washington; they're screwing everything up. What we need are term limits."

This time, Pete greets me with, "Well, look who's here. The defender of the indefensible."

Vince just grunts; he's busy watching the Mets game. When I ask how the game is going, he says, "Mets are getting killed." I look at the screen and see that they're down 2–0 in the second inning; years of pain have turned Vince into something of a pessimist where the Mets are concerned.

I doubt very much that Pete will give me any information about the case against Kramer, but there's no harm in giving it a shot. "Once again, you got the wrong man," I say.

He laughs. "Yeah, right. Because you'll only defend the purest of the pure."

"Actually, I just assume that whoever you arrest is innocent. If you were working the Lincoln assassination, John Wilkes Booth would be on *Dancing with the Stars* today."

He holds up his beer. "I named a drink in your honor; I'm going to have this beer, and then follow it with an ambulance chaser."

"And you can pay for both," I say.

This immediately gets Vince's attention and causes him to turn away from the television. I doubt Vince even brings his wallet with him when he comes here anymore. "Boys, boys . . . let's not let this get out of hand. We're all friends here."

"Well, 'friends' . . . I know you've been charging to my tab even when I'm not here."

Vince fakes a look of shock. "What? I had no idea . . . I thought they were giving us free food and beer because they were paying off the crooked cop here." He points at Pete in case I didn't know which crooked cop he was referring to.

Pete nods. "I for one am stunned that a reputable restaurant would take advantage of you like that. I'm going to commence an immediate, time-consuming investigation. In the meantime, we should proceed as we have been, so they don't get suspicious."

"That's comforting," I say. "But I'm still going to embarrass you in court. Again."

"Color me scared," Pete says. "By the way, didn't Kramer used to go out with Laurie? Before she defied all logic and married you?"

"I believe they went out, yes," I say.

Vince laughs. "That must make for an interesting situation."

"I believe it does, yes," I say.

aurie, Ricky, and I try to have breakfast together every morning. With me not working, that hasn't been too difficult a feat to accomplish. That's going to change; a murder case, if it goes to trial, changes everything. But today we stick to the script, and Laurie makes pancakes, after which Ricky joins Tara, Sebastian, and me on our morning walk.

Before we leave, I say to Laurie, "By the way, Kramer's not married."

She nods. "I know. I assume he figured you'd be more likely to take the case if you thought he was. Your attitude wasn't that friendly when you first met him."

"So you decided to just stand there and stay silent while he lied?"

"I did."

"I thought he was so honest," I say.

"He's not a saint, Andy," she says and smiles.

Laurie doesn't seem upset by my outrage, probably because she knows it's false. If I were in Kramer's position, I would have told the same lie. I might have even added a few kids to my fake family, and maybe a sick mother in a home.

"You'll notify everyone?" I ask.

She nods. "I will."

Because we so rarely take on clients, every time we do so, we need to inform and assemble the defense team. It reminds me of those movies where the old gang gets summoned back for one last job or assignment. Most of them are doing other things and, depending on

the person, are either pleased or displeased to be called back into action. But eventually they all come on board, or there would be no movie.

While we're walking, Ricky asks, "Are you going back to work?"

"Looks like it."

"But if you don't like to work, why are you doing it?"

From the mouths of babes. But I'm in a bit of a tough spot here; I don't want to prejudice Ricky against working. "Working is good; I just like to spend time with you and your mom even more."

"Am I going to have to work when I grow up?"

"You're going to pick the kind of work that you love, so you'll look forward to it."

He nods. "Okay. Sounds good."

I bring Ricky, Tara, and Sebastian back home and then head down to the foundation building. It's only eight thirty, but I've never seen the place busier. In addition to Willie and Sondra, there are at least half a dozen volunteers.

"You got enough help?" I ask Willie.

"More than we need. The story hit the newspapers that we have all these dogs, and people are calling like crazy to volunteer."

"You have them all logged into the system?" I ask. We keep a computer file on every dog we take in.

He nods. "Sondra took care of it. There's one dog that seems to be missing . . . there was a cage on the truck that was empty. There was a card for the dog, but no dog."

"Maybe it was already placed in a home?" I say. "I wouldn't worry too much about it. Willie, about the workload. You know I'm taking on a case, and—"

He interrupts. "Don't worry about it. It's cool."

Willie knows that I feel guilty about him and Sondra doing all the work, but they love it. Willie is a former client; I represented him after he spent seven years on death row. We proved his innocence, got his conviction overturned, and then won a fortune for him in a suit against the real murderers. So he doesn't have to work and is happy to spend his time saving the lives of deserving dogs.

I go into the dog area to visit with the newcomers. I generally grav-

itate to the seniors, and I spend some time petting several of them. But the golden retriever puppies are ridiculously cute. Sondra has named the mother Wiggy, because she has what seems like extra hair on the top of her head. She seems to tolerate the puppies grudgingly and would clearly rather sleep than dote on them.

The dogs are in caged runs, and the volunteers are letting them into the play area in shifts to interact with their traveling buddies. Willie and Sondra are being cautious about it until they make sure that they know which ones are dog-friendly. So far, no issues have cropped up.

I could happily spend the entire day here, but I have to go down to the jail. There it is the humans who are in cages; some are already housed in what will be their "forever home." My task is to make sure that Kramer is not one of those people.

We meet in a room reserved for lawyer-client conferences. Kramer is brought in handcuffed but seems in relatively decent spirits. Many clients, having spent their first night in prison and facing the concept of long-term incarceration, are distraught and panicked. Kramer is much savvier and more experienced, and while I'm sure he's very unhappy with his circumstances, he doesn't seem to want to use emotional capital on things he can't control.

"Start at the beginning," I say.

"I already have. The beginning was when I beat the hell out of Zimmer for molesting my client's daughter."

"Have you had contact with him since that situation was concluded?"

"No, not until a few days ago. He called me out of the blue."

"Why?"

"He said we needed to meet, that there were things to resolve. He said he had information for me that would be helpful to a case I was working on."

"Did he say what case?"

"No, he wouldn't provide any more information. When I asked why he would want to be helpful to me considering our history, he said he would get something out of it as well."

"Did you believe him?" I ask.

"I wouldn't believe him if he told me the sun came up this morning."

"Was there any reason to believe he would have been involved with one of your cases?"

"No. Like I said, I thought he was lying, and I turned out to be right. He never said a word about a case or anything else; he just came out slashing. The story was a pretext so he could kill me."

"Why did you agree to see him?"

"I was curious about it, and I knew that he was someone I could handle if there was a problem."

"And the meeting place was the truck at the rest stop?"

"Right. When I arrived, the truck wasn't there yet. About ten minutes later, it pulled up. I looked in, but there was no one in the driver's seat. I thought he was going to come out, but he didn't. So then I figured he wanted me to come onto the truck and talk to him there."

"So you did?" I ask.

He nods. "Yes, I heard all the dogs barking, which didn't surprise me, because he had told me what he was doing. When I got on the truck, I still didn't see him, so I took a few steps inside. That's when he took a swing at me."

"He tried to punch at you?"

"No. It was a large knife; coming at me, it looked like a damn machete, but it wasn't. He jumped out from behind some kind of partition and tried to slash me in the throat with it. Almost got me the first time, so he wound up to try again."

"What did you do?"

"I shot him," he says and then smiles. "You know what they say; never bring a knife to a gunfight."

"What did you do then?"

"I checked to confirm he was dead, and then I left." When he sees me react slightly to this admission, he says, "I know; big mistake. I should have known better."

"Yes."

"I didn't have a lot of time, and I was pretty shaken up; he's the first man I'd ever killed. Since I had assaulted him once, and . . . did I mention that it was part of the record that I had threatened to kill him?"

"No, you left that part out," I say.

"Well, I did. Considering all that, I thought I might just leave and not be implicated. Then after I did, I realized I had forgotten to see if there were any security cameras installed at the rest stop. I didn't want to drive back there, so I went south to the next rest stop, thinking it would be the same."

"Cameras?" I ask.

He nods. "A single camera. But in a position that it would have seen me. That's when I decided I should talk to you. Laurie and I have kept in touch a bit over the years, so I called her. I told her I was in trouble, and she said to come right over."

The fact that he and Laurie had been in touch is news to me, but not really the point at the moment. "How did the police know you were at my house?"

"I stopped at my place and left a note on the door saying that if anyone was looking for me, that's where I'd be. I figured there was no harm; if by some chance they hadn't ID'd me yet, then they wouldn't see the note. But obviously they had; it wasn't exactly a whodunit."

"Where's the gun?" I ask.

"It was at my house where I left it. My guess is it's in the police lab now getting tests done on the ballistics. Those tests won't come back in my favor."

"It will all be turned over to us."

"I'm in deep shit," he says. "Now what do we do?"

"We start digging you out."

've done this so often, I know what everyone's thinking before we even enter the room.

Laurie and I have driven to my office on Van Houten Street in downtown Paterson for our initial team meeting on the Kramer case. Laurie has rounded them up, and all will be there with the exception of Hike, the other lawyer in my firm, who is out of town. He will participate by phone.

Everyone is in place when we arrive, sitting around the conference table. The air-conditioning is not working well, or really at all, but since we've spent the summer without a client, I haven't been checking to see whether it's been fixed.

It hasn't. The owner of the building is Sofia Hernandez, who owns the fruit stand on the street level . . . we're on the second floor. She probably hasn't gotten around to it because we're never here, and also because this is prime summer fruit season. Sofia has her priorities.

So it's very uncomfortable, even though someone has turned on a couple of fans and opened the windows. The upside is that the smell of fresh cantaloupe is wafting through the window, and I do love cantaloupe. The downside is that it's so hot in here you could fry a cantaloupe on the floor.

The conference table can barely fit in the small room, and everyone looks crowded, hot, and generally miserable. Welcome to the big time.

To my immediate left is Edna, who used to be my secretary. She has given herself promotions in title, initially to administrative assistant and then to office manager. The key thing to know about her work is that she doesn't do anything, and if she did, it would be with great reluctance. She must realize that the fact that we called this meeting means that we have a client, which I am sure she finds horrifying. Edna has the seat closest to the door, because she always wants to be the first one out.

Next to her is Sam Willis, my accountant and neighbor, in that he has an office down the hall. Sam is a computer genius, capable of hacking into absolutely everything, even when the law considers such hacking impermissible. Fortunately, I consider it permissible and take great advantage of his skills when we need them.

Sam hates accounting almost as much as I hate lawyering, so he loves when we have a case. He wants to be in on the action, though his preference would be that he could be working for a SWAT team commander instead of a lawyer.

Next is Willie Miller, not officially a team member but someone whose toughness and reliability often prove very valuable. Willie is the one person in the room other than Laurie and me who knows why we're here, since he was at the murder scene.

Next to Willie is Marcus Clark, whose presence causes me to reconsider my claim that I know what everyone is thinking. I never, absolutely never, know what Marcus is thinking. He is the scariest person on the planet, and the toughest. He has literally saved my life on a number of occasions.

Marcus is also a top-notch investigator, but he almost never talks; he throws around barely decipherable syllables like other people throw around Winnebagos. He and Laurie have a terrific relationship, which I've always assumed is why he allows me to continue living.

There's some noise that is disconcertingly loud; it sounds like people are having a party. I go to the window, thinking it's coming from the street, but it isn't.

Edna points to the phone, which is on speaker. "It's Hike," she says. "Hike?"

Hike's voice comes through the phone. "Andy? You guys ready? Let me get somewhere quiet."

"I think he's at a brunch with a few hundred of his closest friends,"

Edna says, rolling her eyes in a combination of amazement and disdain.

The thing to know about Hike, and I don't want to overstate this, is that he is the most downbeat person in the history of the world. He sees the bad in everything and assumes every situation, no matter how dire, is going to get worse.

But I sent him to South Carolina on a case not long ago, and he just took to it. His entire personality changed; within forty-eight hours, he was the toast of the town, surrounded by newfound friends.

When he came back here, he returned to good old miserable Hike, but he takes occasional trips to South Carolina for enjoyment. I actually never thought I would create a single sentence that included both words *Hike* and *enjoyment*, but there it is.

About thirty seconds later, he comes back on the phone. The background noises are gone. "I'm back. What's up?"

"We've got a client."

"Definitely?" Edna asks, obviously hoping I just forgot to use the word *possible* or *potential* before *client*.

"Definitely. His name is Dave Kramer, and he's accused of killing a man named Kenny Zimmer."

"But he didn't do it?" Sam asks.

"Oh, he did it, but in self-defense," I say and then go on to describe what we know. It isn't much, just basically what Kramer has told us. We haven't gotten any discovery yet; that will come after tomorrow's arraignment.

This meeting is basically just to get everyone aware of, and ready for, the upcoming case. There isn't a lot I can tell them, and there's only the most bare-bones strategy to be formed.

"We're going to have to demonstrate motive for Zimmer to have brought Kramer to the rest stop for the purpose of killing him," I say. "That should not be so difficult because of their prior history. But we'll need to get phone and email records to document Zimmer's contacting him."

Sam nods at this; he will be in charge of getting those records. I might have him do it in his own way, which means not bothering with the legal niceties. If they show what we hope they do, we can then get them legally. If not, the prosecutor doesn't have to know we were going after them.

"The forensics and crime scene material will be crucial; we'll need to prove that our client was defending himself on that truck," I say. "The security video should help in that it will show he didn't draw his gun before he got on."

I continue. "We'll also need to do a deep dive into Zimmer. The worse we can make him look, the better. This is going to be a 'he said, he said,' and the opposition 'he said' guy is dead. Our client has his own issues, especially the assault against Zimmer. But we should be able to get character witnesses on his behalf. Right, Laurie?"

Laurie nods, and I notice that Marcus does as well.

"Absolutely," Laurie says. "Dave has a lot of friends in law enforcement. He's always had their backs, and they will have his."

"Marcus, you know him?" I ask.

There is a pause of about fifteen seconds. Marcus sometimes holds conversations as if he is on tape delay, yet I know for a fact that he is whip-smart and capable of amazing split-second decisions. Finally, he says, "Yunh."

With a ringing endorsement like that, how can we lose?

"Who is the prosecutor?" Hike asks through the phone.

"Don't know yet," I say. "I'll find out after we're done here. Anybody have any questions?"

Nobody does, so I guess we are, in fact, "done here." I tell everyone that I will update them as soon as I know more and am ready to give out specific assignments.

Once we break up the meeting, Laurie and I head back home. Anything I have to do, I can do from there. In fact, the need to have an office at all has lessened over time to the point where it's an unnecessary luxury, if you can call a stiflingly hot dump over a fruit stand a luxury. But it somehow feels like I should keep the office, if for no other reason than to give Edna a place not to go to every day.

On the way home, I ask, "How does Marcus know Kramer?"

"He did some investigative work for him maybe five years ago, after Dave left the force," she says. "And . . ."

She doesn't seem inclined to go any further, and since *and* is not a complete sentence, I prompt her. "And . . . ?"

"And we all went out a couple of times."

"You, Marcus, and Kramer?"

"And Marcus's wife."

I've only met Marcus's wife once, at a victory party after a successful case. She referred to him as her "little Markie."

"Isn't that nice," I say. "Where did you go? Bowling? Ice-skating? Karaoke?"

"Andy, you need to get past this. I had a life pre-Andy, hard as that may be for you to believe."

"How come we never go out with Marcus and his wife?"

"Would you like to?" she asks.

"Not particularly."

When we get home, I take Tara and Sebastian for a walk in Eastside Park. It gives me a chance to discuss with Tara my attitude toward Kramer. "I'm having trouble getting past this," I say. "It bugs me that this guy was with Laurie."

Tara doesn't say anything, for a couple of reasons. For one, she knows that I need to deal with this on my own; that's the only way I'll get to a resolution. The other reason is that she is a dog, and dogs can't talk . . . not even Tara.

So I continue uninterrupted. "I don't know why I'm jealous of this guy; I know how Laurie feels about me. I mean, look at you; when Sebastian came to live with us, you just took it in stride. You knew how we felt about you, so you dealt with it." As I'm saying this, Sebastian is pissing on a garbage can and doesn't seem like a dog that Tara would have jealous pangs over.

"Okay," I say. "I'm going to play it your way. You're not threatened by Sebastian, and I'm not threatened by Kramer. And if things change, I'll just intentionally lose the case and let him spend the rest of his miserable life in jail. Then if Laurie wants to 'stay in touch' with him, they can whisper sweet nothings through the glass in the prison visiting room."

With that resolved, I take the dogs home and call the prosecutor's office to find out who will be handling the Kramer case. I'm told it is Carla Westrum, a relative newcomer to the office. She moved here from the West Coast and is highly thought of, though I haven't gone up against her yet.

"Carla?" Laurie asks when I tell her who the prosecutor is. "Really?"

"You know her?" I ask.

"We went to college together. I heard she was in town, but I didn't realize she was working in the prosecutor's office. I haven't talked to her in years, but we've emailed."

"This case is like old home week for you."

"Unfortunately, she's smart, Andy. And she's one of the hardest workers you'll ever come across."

"Super."

"It gets worse. She's also the single most competitive person I've ever met. She was this really nice, normal human being until she got on the volleyball court or the tennis court, and then she became a driven maniac."

"Does Kramer know her also?" I'm asking because if Carla and Kramer have any kind of relationship and it's not revealed to the court, it might be something to use on appeal. It would be a long shot, and I certainly don't want to be in position to have to appeal anything, but it's worth filing away for possible future use.

"Not that I'm aware of," Laurie says.

"You didn't triple date with her and the Marcuses?"

"Andy," she says, showing her uncanny ability to make my name sound like a reprimand.

I decide not to talk to Carla yet; I want to know more about the case first. I'll meet her at the arraignment but will hold off discussing particulars with her until I get a look at the discovery. She might expect us to try to plea bargain it down, but it doesn't seem like Kramer is prepared to do that. And if he really killed Zimmer in self-defense, then I don't blame him. Of course, that's a big if.

Besides, before I do anything else, it's time to visit the scene.

U sually, when I visit a murder scene, it's my first time there. In this case, of course, I was at the rest stop where Zimmer died not long after it happened. I didn't get on to the truck, but I'm hoping to do that today.

Laurie comes with me, as she always does. She has a trained investigator's eye; I have a trained lawyer's eye. Which means I'm better at looking at depositions and briefs, and she's better at crime scenes.

The rest stop is closed and guarded by two cops when we arrive. I'm not sure what these two guys did to wind up getting stuck sitting at a rest stop in the heat all day, but my guess is they are not on the fast track for promotions.

I had called Pete and gotten his approval to enter the scene. He was reluctant to give it, mainly because it goes against his grain to do anything for any defense attorneys anywhere. But he knew we could get permission from the court, and he also knew that if he refused, I would use it to show bias when I eventually get him on the witness stand.

The truck is scheduled to be moved out of here in a few days; I'm told that the owner has been pushing to get possession back. I'm going to want to talk to him to learn whatever he knows about Zimmer and whether or not he has any insight into what happened here.

The cops guarding the crime scene have been alerted to our arrival. They're young guys who must be reasonably new to the department, which is why Laurie doesn't know them. She's been off the force for quite a few years now, so there is an increasing number of officers who she is unfamiliar with.

The truck obviously hasn't been moved and therefore is still positioned awkwardly in terms of parking. I can see fingerprint dust on the door to the restroom and on the truck's door handle, but it doesn't matter to me whether or not they found Kramer's prints. We are not going to contend that he was not here; that's not our defense.

"Where did Dave park?" Laurie asks.

"I'm not sure."

She nods. "Either way, the camera got him." She points to a video camera above and to the left of the restroom door; there is no doubt that the truck's door is in the range of the camera.

"That's obviously how they knew to go to his house," I say.

We climb the two steps to the entrance to the truck's interior. I let Laurie go first. It has nothing to do with chivalry; murder scenes still creep me out. She shows no hesitation, and I follow her in.

We walk all the way through, gingerly stepping over Zimmer's dried blood and police chalk marks. We don't want to mess anything up, though obviously the place has been thoroughly photographed and catalogued.

The setup is excellent in terms of the dogs; there are at least seventy cages, all clean and comfortable, with cushioned dog beds and water dishes in each. The dogs were traveling in style, and whoever arranged all this cared about their comfort and safety.

The truck is set up in three sections. Moving back from the driver's seat, there is a room with maybe twenty cages on each side, and a fairly large open pathway between them. Then there is a large room with heavily padded walls. Beyond that is another dog area, this time with what looks to be at least forty cages. It is similar to the other dog area.

"The padded area must be where they let the dogs out of their cages to play," Laurie says. "The pads would prevent them from crashing into walls if the truck swerved."

"Makes sense to me," I say.

Laurie points to a partition near where the bloodstains are. "That's where Zimmer hid before he attacked Dave. He came out of there swinging the knife. Dave backed away, probably just a few feet, and shot. The forensics should tell us how far away he was."

"The closer the better," I say. If he shot from a long distance, that would impact our self-defense approach. You don't fear for your life from a knife if you're twenty feet away from it. We will have to deal with Kramer's use of deadly force; the prosecution will contend that he could have just run off the truck, but he chose instead to fire at Zimmer. We'll have to show that Zimmer was continuing to come after him.

She nods. "Right. The knife isn't here."

"I'm sure they took it to analyze it for prints and trace evidence. They'll have taken pictures of it where they found it."

"Right," she says. "And Zimmer's prints will be on it, which works very much in our favor."

"Unless he was wearing gloves."

"In this heat?" she asks. "He wouldn't have worried about prints, because he would have thought he'd be alive to ditch the weapon. And the prints will be compelling; there's no logical reason for him to have been holding a knife like that, especially if it was lying on the floor, unless he was using it as a weapon."

"They could claim he grabbed it in self-defense or because he was worried about Kramer's arrival. The fact is, a lot of these answers will be in the discovery," I say. "But the knife does seem like a strange choice of weapon."

She nods. "I know. A gun would obviously have been more effective. And then he could have shot Dave when he got out of his car; there was no reason to let him get that close."

"Maybe he wanted it to be more personal," I say.

The truth is that the case seems fairly straightforward and the actions of the players uncomplicated. Zimmer lured Kramer onto the truck, tried to kill him, and came in second place. Now all we have to do is prove it.

They had code names for each other—*Brady* and *Rodgers*.

It was the idea of the man who took the name *Rodgers*, obviously a football fan, and a Packers fan at that. He was in charge, so he gave himself the name he liked best.

Everybody that Rodgers dealt with had a quarterback code name, and Brady went along for a few reasons. There was no reason not to play along; it seemed like a harmless bit of drama.

Another reason he went along was that Rodgers was calling the shots; Rodgers called all the shots. To cross Rodgers, to even express more than mild disagreement with Rodgers, was to take a great personal risk. Brady, it must be said, was generally risk averse.

The final reason he went along is that Rodgers had already made him very, very rich.

"He hired a lawyer named Carpenter," Brady said when Rodgers called him. This was not exactly a revelation; Carpenter's hiring was in the newspapers this morning.

"Tell me something I don't know," Rodgers said.

"I don't have anything yet. But I'm worried."

"Carpenter won't have anything to work with," Rodgers pointed out. "You have nothing to worry about; your job is finished."

"I was surprised you didn't kill Kramer," Brady said. He said it cautiously in a tone that avoided judgment. He had to tread very carefully with Rodgers.

"It could have worked out that way, but it didn't. Doesn't matter;

this is just as good. Maybe better." That was what he said to Brady, but the truth is he was very upset over the incident with Kramer. It was the man known as Manning's doing, and it was a serious over-reaction. Kramer could and should have been left alone; what happened called more attention to them, not less.

He had told Manning that and insisted that any such actions be cleared with him in the future. Kramer was simply not a serious threat, at least not in the short term. And there would be no long term to worry about.

"Okay, you know best," Brady said.

"Yeah. I do. All good on your end?"

"Absolutely."

"Good," Rodgers said. Then, since Rodgers could hear the nervousness in Brady's voice, he added, "Relax. All you need to do is count your money."

arla Westrum is really tall, at least six foot two. That's the first thing I notice about her when she graciously comes over to introduce herself at this arraignment. Maybe it's because height is becoming a recurring theme in this case. Kramer could be a shooting guard in the NBA, and Laurie, who is sitting just behind me, is five eleven and a quarter. Since I am about five ten with no quarter, I'm starting to feel like I'm walking among the trees.

Carla is also quite attractive; not Laurie-attractive, but nobody besides Laurie is. Between the two of them and Kramer, I'm lamenting my lack of both height and good looks.

I am reminded of a *Twilight Zone* episode in which everybody living in a particular place or planet was horribly ugly, except for one woman who was beautiful. But because of the prevailing standard, the beautiful one was considered ugly, and the ugly were revered as beautiful. It was a world in which everything was therefore reversed.

Rod Serling, where are you now when I need you most?

Fortunately, I don't actually need old Rod, because I turn and see Hike sitting at the defense table, and I immediately feel better. I'm not alone.

Carla tells me that the discovery documents are in the process of being transferred to us, adding that at this point the material is rather skimpy, because the case is just getting started. "Maybe it's skimpy because you have no case," I say, and she just laughs. It is not a worried laugh.

She sees Laurie and brightens immediately. She goes to her and they hug and start to talk, probably making plans to get together after she sends my client to prison for the rest of his life. Then the judge comes in, and Carla goes back to the prosecution table, where the rest of her team is already in place.

Kramer gives me a questioning look, no doubt curious about the Laurie-Carla reunion.

I shrug. "They went to school together."

The judge is Arthur Avery, and while I won't go so far as to say it's a break for the defense, it certainly could be worse. I've tried two cases in front of Judge Avery, and I've found him to be smart and reasonably fair. He also is decisive; he makes rulings quickly, confidently, and usually correctly.

But the most positive aspect of his drawing the case is he's more willing than most judges to tolerate my bullshit. He doesn't like me; they haven't invented the judge who likes me. But he doesn't seem to hate me as much as some of his colleagues, which gives me a warm, fuzzy feeling.

We all rise when Judge Avery enters. He tells the bailiff to read the number and nature of the case and then turns the floor over to Carla. This is going to be a by-the-book arraignment, which is almost always the way it works.

Carla recites the basics of the case, which consist of the fact that the State of New Jersey believes that David Kramer willfully and with premeditation caused the death of Kenneth Zimmer. She reveals that the charge is first-degree murder and asks that Kramer be held without bail.

Judge Avery turns to us and asks how the defendant pleads. Kramer answers in a firm, confident voice, "Not guilty, Your Honor." Judge Avery sets a date for trial, which is considerably sooner than I'd like, but I go along with it. This is a self-defense case and is relatively uncomplicated; I have no doubt we will be ready. If we're not, it won't be because of inadequate time to prepare.

I raise the issue of bail, though we have no chance of prevailing. We can't even argue that Kramer has never before been accused of a violent crime. Not only has he been convicted of assault, but it was an assault against the victim in this case.

Judge Avery denies the request, as I warned Kramer that he would. The judge ends the arraignment with a quick pound of his gavel, and the bailiff comes to take Kramer away.

Just before he leaves, he simply says, "Keep me posted, please."

I promise that I will.

Hike tells me that the discovery documents, such as they are, should be at our office, so that's where Laurie and I are going next. I want to see whatever forensic reports are available, as well as the photographs that were taken. We're going to have to reconstruct the crime, based on this information, in a way that is favorable to our client.

So Laurie and I head down to the office. Sofia Hernandez greets us at the entrance with an apology for the delay in fixing the air conditioner and a pound of cherries to make up for it. It's a reasonable trade.

But since it feels like it's about four thousand degrees in the office, and since we have to pick Ricky up from his friend Will Rubenstein's house soon, we load the documents into the car. This way we'll be able to read them in air-conditioned comfort while I suck down the cherries.

We get Ricky, and Will comes along also for a sleepover. It's a misnamed event, since they rarely get any sleep. Tara and Sebastian love when both kids are at our house, since it means four hands for petting.

We have dinner, and it's almost seven o'clock when I settle in the den to go through the documents. First, I look at the forensic reports, which at this point are unremarkable. One thing in our favor is the information on the bullet's entry into the body, where the casings were found, and the gunpowder residue.

It should be easy to make the case that Kramer was less than five feet away from Zimmer when he fired the fatal shot. And that helps us in our claim of self-defense; he was well within range of Zimmer swinging the knife.

There is no information about the knife in the forensics; that obviously has not been completed yet. But I'm very interested to know where the knife was found, so I start in on the photographs. There are seventy-five of them, a huge amount considering the murder scene was so confined.

I've gone through all seventy-five before I am ready to accept one devastating fact.

There is no knife.

T hat's simply not possible, Andy."

That's what I expect Laurie to say when I tell her about the lack of a knife in the photographs, and that's exactly what she says.

"I've looked through the photos twice, and it's not there. You can look for yourself."

"Is it referred to in the forensic reports?" she asks.

"I've only looked through them quickly, but I didn't see it. I'm pretty sure the answer is no."

"How can that be?"

"Well, maybe there was an accomplice of Zimmer's there, and he chose to leave and take it with him," I say.

She shakes her head. "Doesn't make sense, for a number of reasons. Dave didn't see anyone else, and Zimmer's accomplice would probably have helped him kill Dave rather than stand by while Dave killed Zimmer."

"Right. Another possibility is that the police removed it, to set up Kramer for the murder."

"Pete?" she asks, eyebrows raised. "You know better than that."

I nod. "Yes, I do. Which brings us to the option behind door number three."

Another shake of her head, this time more insistent. "No."

"Laurie, we have to at least face the possibility that there was no knife, that Kramer made the whole thing up."

"No," she repeats.

"The story didn't make sense in the first place. Zimmer should have assumed that Kramer was armed, and at the very least, he should have known he'd be tough to handle. Kramer beat him up once before, remember?"

"I'm not buying it," she says.

"Why? Because you like him? Because you trust him? If you take your personal feelings out of it and look at the facts we're presented with, you can't come up with any other conclusion."

"I am looking at the facts. Dave is smart, and more than that, he spent most of his career in law enforcement. He knows how crime scenes are handled, and he would know that if he made up this story, it would instantly be exposed as bull. There would be no chance the story would be believed and, therefore, no upside in telling it."

It's a good point, but I'm not going to accept it without a fight. "Maybe he panicked."

"Panicked?" she asks. "He didn't get caught in the act and blurt something out. He would have had time to plan the crime, and then plenty of time afterward to make up a story. He practically invited the cops to arrest him; he left them a damn note. He had ample opportunity to come up with something much better."

"Will you admit it's the most likely of our three possible explanations?"

She nods. "I will, but that's a low bar to go over. There's a fourth explanation that we haven't seen yet, and it's the one that's true."

I go back to the discovery documents in the hope that I will find phone records that show the contact between Zimmer and Kramer. Their meeting was set up; Kramer didn't just happen to wander to the rest stop where Zimmer's truck was parked. Kramer said that Zimmer had contacted him, and I need to confirm that it is true.

It is significant in that if Kramer initiated the contact, we are in big trouble. It would be easy for the prosecution to argue that he did so to set up Zimmer to be killed.

If Zimmer made the call, then he could have done so to set Kramer up so that he could kill him with the now-missing knife. Or he could have had another motive, and it might have been the revelation of that motive that caused Kramer to shoot him. If that's the case, Kramer hasn't revealed what that motive is. His position is that Zimmer lured him into a trap.

The records are not here, which is not a big deal, since Sam Willis is getting them for me by hacking in the phone company's computers. I should have them by tomorrow.

My default position is usually to believe my clients; in fact, I no longer take cases in which I don't believe in their innocence. In this case, I have strong doubts, though I recognize that those doubts may be partially fueled by my petty jealousies. Is there such a thing as a non-petty jealousy?

If I get to the point where I absolutely believe that Kramer is guilty of murder, I am going to drop him as a client. I'll find him a good attorney if he wants me to, but it won't be me.

That is nonnegotiable.

I'll just have to find someone to tell Laurie.

hate visiting clients in jail. Maybe I should have thought of that before I became a criminal defense attorney, because jail is where most of my clients hang out. I should have been a sports agent, so I could hang out in stadiums. Or a travel agent, so I could . . . you get the picture.

But as the late, great Hyman Roth said, "This is the business we have chosen." I never got the feeling that Hyman regretted his choice as much as I have. I became a criminal attorney because my father was a respected member of the justice system as a district attorney. I don't have a clue what Hyman's father did.

Today is Labor Day, an added irony as I ponder my occupation while waiting to be let in to speak to Kramer. Maybe *speak* is the wrong word; *confront* might be more accurate. But we'll see; I'm more comfortable with speaking than confronting. I'm more comfortable with a lot of things than confronting.

But I do it, because this is the business I've chosen.

Kramer is brought into the attorney visiting room, and I guess he is good at judging faces, because the first thing he says is, "You aren't here with good news."

"I would say that's probably accurate."

"Let's hear it."

I nod. "We got the initial discovery documents, which include some of the forensics and all of the photographs of the crime scene."

"And?"

"No knife. No reference to it, no photograph of it, nothing."

He doesn't say anything for at least fifteen seconds as he digests it. He either knows there never was a knife and is therefore not surprised, or he knows there was and is shocked. I try to read his face and come to the conclusion that I don't have the vaguest idea as to what he's thinking.

But he says, "That's simply not possible." Which are exactly the words Laurie used.

"We're not dealing in possibilities," I say. "We're dealing in fact. When the police arrived, there was no weapon."

"And when I left, there was," Kramer says. "Pete wouldn't have ditched it; it's not his style. And he wouldn't have any reason to do so, or at least none that I know of. Besides, at that point, he couldn't even have known I was involved."

"Right."

"Which means someone else was there. Someone else had to take it."

"That doesn't make a lot of sense either."

He suspects where I might be going with this. "Nor does me making up the story," he says.

"I'm aware of that."

Suddenly, he slams the table with his cuffed hands. "Damn! Somebody is setting me up! They're trying to take my life away!"

It's a surprising show of emotion from someone who has so far seemed amazingly cool and collected considering his situation. He's obviously realizing what he's up against.

He calms down as quickly as he erupted. "Have you seen the video yet?" he asks.

He's referring to the security camera that covered the area where the truck was parked. If someone took the knife and left, the video should have captured it. "No, it wasn't part of the first round of discovery. But it will be interesting to see."

"You don't believe me?" he asks, though it is as much a statement and a question.

"Doesn't matter what I believe," I say, lying through my teeth.

"Come on. Of course it does."

"I don't have an explanation for this, but I don't think you're dumb enough to have made up a story that could be so easily shown to be total bullshit."

He smiles, now fully in control again. "My eyes are filling with tears."

I return the smile. "Glad we could share this special moment."

"Have you talked to the prosecutor yet?" he asks.

"She called me this morning, but I haven't called back yet. Wanted to talk to you first."

"I'm not pleading it out," he says. "I'm not letting them win without a fight."

"Okay."

"It looks bad now, but I did not commit a murder. I'm not going to say I did."

I nod and stand up. "I'll get back to you."

I turn to leave and then stop. "Let's assume for a moment that you were set up, that there was someone on that truck. Or someone that showed up after you left and removed the weapon. It makes this more than a revenge move by Zimmer; it means someone else wanted you out of the way."

"Right."

"So who might that be, and why?"

He pauses. "Something for me to think about."

"Think hard," I say. "And write your thoughts down. I'll be waiting."

I start heading home and then take a detour toward the rest stop on the Garden State Parkway. I haven't been to highway rest stops this often since my aunt Mary in Philadelphia accidentally used spoiled milk in the bread pudding on Thanksgiving when I was twelve.

The truck is still here, and the same two poor cops are guarding it. They recognize me, but not with a smile. I don't ask for permission to enter, I just do so, and they don't try to stop me. I guess Pete's instructions to grant me entry are still in effect.

I board the truck and go to the back to check and see what the rear exit is like. Not only is there a large door, typical of a tractor trailer, which raises from the bottom to the top, but there is also a more traditional door with three steps that can be lowered down from it. It would have been easy for someone to exit from back here.

I also check and see that there are two storage rooms we didn't notice before, where someone easily could have hidden. They contain mostly pet supplies, and there are no signs that the cops dusted for prints back here. I make a mental note to ask for it to be done.

I exit the truck through the back door and walk through the woods out to the highway. Then I loop around and come back through the automobile entrance. The cops seem surprised to see me; they hadn't realized I had left.

Next, I go toward where the security camera is, to see what it covers. I'm unable to tell exactly because it is so high up, and I can't see what it sees and what it doesn't. I'll know when I get the video.

On the way home, I call Pete and ask for the rooms to be checked for prints. I also tell him that I was just at the scene, and I want a copy of the security camera tape for the past two hours.

"Why should I do all this, Sherlock?"

"Because I asked you to. And because you are dedicated to truth and justice. And because if you don't, I'll ask for a court order. And because I'll point out that you wouldn't do it on your own when I get you on the stand. And because I will never buy you another beer in your entire stinking, wretched life."

"Done," he says.

The video isn't a disaster, and at this point, disaster avoidance feels like a triumph. It arrived this morning along with more discovery, and while it doesn't show the presence of anyone else who might have been on the truck, it doesn't preclude the possibility.

The way the truck was positioned relative to the camera, it is possible that someone exited through the back and was shielded by the truck itself as that person made an escape. Taking the view most favorable to our side, the strange way the truck was parked could have been intentionally placed there so as to do that shielding.

That's the relatively good news. Part of the bad news is that everything is ambiguous enough that I am stuck on this case; I don't really have grounds to withdraw. I'm of course not talking about grounds to present to the court; I'm talking about making a case to Laurie.

I am a tower of legal jelly.

The really bad news is that our self-defense case just went down the drain. We have a victim who previously was beaten up by our client, and we would be contending that he attacked our client without being able to show he had a weapon. Even if we could get a jury to believe that, they'd never buy that Kramer needed to shoot and kill him to save himself. It just wouldn't fly.

So we are going to have to claim that this was a well-orchestrated attempt to frame Kramer for murder. Of course, that has its own logical problem. Was Zimmer trying to frame Kramer for his own murder?

Strange way to commit suicide. And if not him, then who? We have no idea.

Kramer said that Zimmer took a solid swing at him with a deadly weapon. I have to assume that Zimmer was trying to connect, which means that Zimmer was trying to kill him, not frame him.

Zimmer's accomplice, whoever that might have been, could have had a backup plan. He would either watch Zimmer kill Kramer, or if Kramer prevailed, frame him for Zimmer's death. It had to be planned in advance; the decision to take the knife and escape while shielded from the camera by the truck was not a spur-of-the-moment move.

If I'm right, then under this scenario, Zimmer's partner would win as long as someone on that truck wound up dead. If I'm wrong, then Laurie's ex-boyfriend is a cold-blooded murderer, and I always hoped she had better taste in men than that.

At the very least, we have a new strategy to pursue. It's not necessary to call another meeting; there's no sense upsetting Edna. The only person besides Laurie and me that needs to know the strategy is Hike, so I call him and ask him to come over to the house.

"Okay," he says, reluctance oozing from his mouth. "Can I bring Darlene?"

"Who's Darlene?"

"My fiancée."

This statement would ordinarily make me drop the phone, but I'm talking hands-free in the car, so there is no phone to drop. "Did I get a wrong number? Is this Hike Lynch? The lawyer?"

"What do you mean?"

"Hike, you've never mentioned a fiancée. You've never mentioned a girlfriend. You've never mentioned a woman at all."

"I met her in South Carolina. We hit it off. She makes me laugh."

I've never heard Hike laugh. I've heard him moan, and whine, and mutter, but I didn't know he had "laugh" in his repertoire. "Hike, definitely bring her," I say. "I want to meet the woman who makes you laugh."

When I get home, I update Laurie on what I've learned, or more accurately, haven't learned. She subscribes to the "third person on the truck" theory; she would subscribe to the "tooth fairy is the killer" theory rather than admit the possibility that Kramer could be the murderer.

"Oh, Willie called," she says. "He's gone over all the records for the dogs that were on the truck. He doesn't see anything relating to rescue groups or people up here that were waiting for them."

"Okay. I'm going to see the guy who owns the truck tomorrow."

I tell Laurie that Hike is coming over with his fiancée, and she seems to take it in stride. He apparently had previously mentioned it to her. "She makes him laugh," Laurie says.

Hike and Darlene arrive in about fifteen minutes. Darlene has a weak, hesitant smile and maybe seems a little nervous as she holds on to Hike's arm while he introduces us. She's wearing a light jacket, which seems a bit strange in the ninety-degree weather, and I offer to take it for her.

"No, thank you, I have a chill."

I'm surprised by this. We have the air-conditioning on in the house, but it's so warm out that it's having trouble keeping up. "Would you like me to turn down the air-conditioning?" I ask.

"That would be nice, thank you," she says, surprising me and leaving me sorry I offered.

"I'll do it," Laurie says and walks over to the thermostat and does so. Then she says, "Darlene, why don't you and I go in the den while Andy and Hike talk about the case?"

"That would be nice, thank you."

She starts to follow Laurie into the den but stops short when she sees Tara and Sebastian in there. "Oh, you have dogs?"

"Yes," Laurie says. "Do you have a dog?"

"No. I had a bad experience with one when I was little, at my grandmother's house."

"Were you bitten?" I ask.

"No," she says, but she seems disinclined to provide further information. Maybe she and the dog argued over politics or sports.

Hike jumps in. "Andy loves dogs."

"Oh," Darlene says and turns to me. "Why?"

I don't answer; I need to cut this off. Darlene makes Hike look like Jimmy Kimmel.

I take Tara and Sebastian into the kitchen with Hike while Laurie heads into the den with laugh-a-minute Darlene. I want to get this over with before the un-air-conditioned house hits 112 degrees.

Hike agrees with the strategy, though he clearly thinks that Kramer is guilty. He almost always thinks our clients are guilty, and even when he doesn't, he thinks we're going to lose.

Once we're done, he says, "So what do you think of Darlene?"

"Seems very nice," I say. "And she makes you laugh. When are you getting married?"

"Haven't set a date yet," he says.

"Will you live up here or down there?"

He shrugs. "Don't know that either. We haven't made real plans yet. Right now, we're just having fun and loving life."

"It won't always be all fun and games and wild living, Hike. Someday, you'll settle down in a house in the suburbs . . . you, Darlene, two kids, no air-conditioning, and no dog."

'd offered to meet at George Davenport's office, but he said he doesn't have one. So instead he suggested a coffee shop in a strip mall on Route 4, about ten minutes from my house. When I enter, a man I assume is Davenport is sitting at a booth near the back, with a cup of coffee and a laptop computer in front of him. The reason I assume it's him is that there are only three patrons in the place, and the other two are women.

Davenport is a big guy; he looks like he was shoehorned into the bench against the wall. When I walk toward him, he says, "Carpenter?"

"That's me."

He reaches to shake my hand. "George Davenport."

I sit across from him and order coffee from the waiter who has come over. "I've seen you on television," he says.

I've been in the media fairly often on high-profile cases. "I look even better in person, don't you think?" I ask.

He laughs. "If you say so. So you're the lawyer for the guy that murdered Zimmer?"

"I'm the lawyer for the guy accused of murdering Zimmer."

He nods. "Right. My mistake."

"What can you tell me about the late Mr. Zimmer?"

He shrugs. "Truth is I don't know that much about him. I placed an ad in that Craigslist thing, and he applied. I met with him, checked to make sure he had a license to drive a rig, and hired him."

"How long ago?'

"About four weeks. Maybe five. I could check."

"How often did he bring dogs up for you?"

"Every other week. I've got two drivers. They alternate weeks," he says. "This was Zimmer's third run. Of course, now I don't have my truck, because the cops haven't released it yet."

"So what were Zimmer's responsibilities?"

"He had a list of shelters down South; it's pretty bad for unwanted animals down there. He'd call and make arrangements to get the dogs that they wanted to send up North. Then he had a list of shelters and rescue groups up here that would take the dogs, and he just matched them up."

"Then he'd drive from here?"

He nods. "Right. He'd leave on a Tuesday, spend a couple of days down there making stops, and head back up North to make whatever stops he had set up."

"You make money doing this?" I ask.

"You make money as a lawyer? It's what I do; it's my occupation."

"So it's not about the dogs?"

He seems a bit insulted by this. "Hey, I'm saving the damn dogs, aren't I? But at the end of the day, they're dogs, right? And dogs are dogs."

"You have a pen?" I ask. "Because I want to write that down; it's really profound." I pretend to write. "Dogs are dogs."

He ignores the sarcasm. "So I'm doing a good thing, but I'm providing a service, and I'm getting paid for it."

"You mind if I ask how much?"

"A hundred fifty a pop."

"Not bad; not bad at all. Who pays the money?"

"The rescue groups that receive them. Then they charge the families that wind up taking them an adoption fee, so that makes them whole. So people wind up fine, and the dogs do even better."

"Do your drivers tell you where they are getting the dogs and dropping them off for each trip?" I ask.

"Sure. They email me a list."

"There were no records on Zimmer's truck about any drop-offs he had arranged."

"There had to be," he says. "He must have been keeping track some-how."

"Did he email you?"

He shrugs. "Let's see." He starts typing into the computer and after a minute says, "That's weird. Never got it. First time that's happened."

"Any idea why?"

"None. You think the dogs have something to do with him get-ting killed?"

"I'm just gathering the facts," I say, but the truth is I do not believe the dogs could have had anything to do with any of this. How could they have? I think Zimmer had a lot on his mind, and planning to confront and maybe kill Kramer would have been his first priority. Doing paperwork would have taken a distant back seat to that.

"So according to the newspaper, you have the dogs now?" he asks.

"I do."

"Technically, they're my dogs."

"Yet I have them," I say. "Technically and literally."

"You going to pay me for them?"

"Did you pay for them?"

He shrugs. "No."

"Then, to use your phrase, you're already 'whole.'"

"I could sue you," he says.

"Clearly you are unaware of my legal prowess."

"This doesn't seem right."

"I hear you, but it's a dog-eat-dog world out there," I say.

R odgers saw himself as chairman of a very unique board. There were two other working members besides himself, each one with an operating name of an NFL quarterback. Besides himself, there was Manning and Elway. Rodgers didn't think it was necessary to distinguish between Peyton and Eli, so Manning was just Manning. There were other people that Rodgers called on to perform individual tasks, but they were dispensable.

In fact, Rodgers considered everyone but himself to be dispensable.

The members of the board each had their own unique skills, and if they weren't the best at what they did, they were damn close. Rodgers had already called on each one a number of times to perform very specific functions, and neither had failed him yet.

Which was good for them, because failure was unacceptable.

The board and its members operated without oversight, either by the government or anyone else. They functioned in a shadow world, with only Rodgers fully aware of the various projects and functions they were undertaking.

Financing was important but was absolutely not an issue. Rodgers had more than enough money to do what had to be done, and that included paying the board members extraordinarily well. There was no other board in the world that paid anywhere close to what these people made, but then again, no other board in the world took these kinds of risks.

Dave Kramer represented a collateral issue to Rodgers. He was not even someone that had to be handled; the fact that Manning had acted independently to do so annoyed him and was a break of established procedure.

Rodgers would keep an eye on the Kramer situation and the machinations of his lawyer, Carpenter. But neither of them represented a significant problem.

And if that changed, the board would handle it. If necessary, the chairman himself would do the job.

t's a mixed bag," Sam says.

I'm generally not a fan of mixed bags; I like my verbal bags pure and positive, especially when Sam is doing the talking. He usually takes the optimistic side of things, so "mixed" coming from him sounds worse than, say, coming from Hike. In Hike's eyes, winning the lottery would be a mixed bag.

"Okay, let's hear it."

"You want the good stuff or the not-so-good stuff first?"

"I'm in your hands, Sam. But can we move it along? It's a bit warm in here." We're in my office, which is down the hall from Sam's, and Sofia Hernandez still hasn't managed to get the air-conditioning fixed. She told me the technical issue involved, but I wouldn't have understood what she was saying even if she were saying it in English, which she was not.

"Okay. I checked into phone contacts between Zimmer and Kramer. Which wasn't so easy, because Zimmer didn't have a phone."

"He didn't have a phone?" I ask. "Who doesn't have a phone?"

"This guy was living in the eighteenth century. No phone, no email address, no computer trail, nothing. But in this case, I should probably just say he didn't have a phone in his name."

"Did he have one in somebody else's name?"

Sam shrugs. "Who knows? I'd have to have the possible name first."

"So we can't show that Zimmer called our client?"

"Not yet. But we can make some assumptions."

I don't like the sound of that, since I've never actually met a judge who was inclined to admit assumptions as evidence. "Make some," I say.

"Well, Kramer got a call a week ago from a burner phone. It was purchased without a contract in a convenience store in Little Rock, Arkansas. The call lasted four minutes. Then he got another call the day before the murder from the same phone. GPS records show the call came from a small town in northern Virginia. That call also lasted four minutes."

Since we know that Zimmer was making dog pickups down South and then working his way north, the geography seems to fit. Zimmer was on the move, and so was the burner phone. It's an assumption, but it sounds like a solid one.

"Hold on a second," I say.

I take out the inventory listed in the discovery documents and see that there is no mention of a cell phone. It would be there if Zimmer was carrying one or if there was one on the truck.

"Can we find out who purchased the phone?" I ask.

"I can't answer that. Somebody would have to check with the store owner personally; it's not on a computer where I can access it. Besides, generally those kinds of purchases are made in cash."

I make a note to ask Kramer to try to figure out exactly when he received the phone calls. I don't want to tell him when they were made; I want him to come up with matching times independently. It's probably another sign of distrust on my part.

"What else have you got?" I ask.

"Well, I did a preliminary rundown on Zimmer. I checked a lot of databases, but I didn't have to check Boy Scout records, because he wasn't one."

That's what passes for a Sam Willis joke, so I fake smile my appreciation, and he moves on.

"I can't find where he ever worked at a job longer than three months. Moved around a lot, mostly on the East Coast, but went as far west as Ohio. He probably didn't like it there, because he was arrested twice."

"What for?"

"Shoplifting once and assault. He was in a bar fight. Charges were dropped in both cases, though I don't see why. I'm sure I can find out."

"Any other arrests?"

"Three. But only one stuck; the last one."

"Tell me about that," I say.

"Three months ago, he was arrested for assault again, but this time the victim wound up in the hospital, and charges weren't dropped. Zimmer was still awaiting trial when he was killed."

"Where was this?" I ask.

"Ocean City, New Jersey."

"So he was out on bail?"

He smiles. "Here comes the good part of the mixed bag. He put up fifty thousand in cash and hired a lawyer who does not come cheap. He gave him a $25,000 retainer."

"You broke into Zimmer's bank account?" It's the only way Sam could know the lawyer retainer figure; those records are confidential and privileged.

He shrugs. "I figured you wouldn't mind."

"Good figuring. Where did he get that kind of money? From working odd jobs?"

"Not unless he got a job as a wire transfer receiver. Right before he made bail, he got seventy-five grand wired into his account from an offshore account in the Caymans that can't be traced."

Sam gives me copies of whatever information he has on Zimmer, including his most recent address. I thank him and head home to discuss all of this with Laurie. I'll also be able to think more clearly when I'm out of this office; it is sauna hot in here.

I relate the information to Laurie in the same order that Sam gave it to me. She stops me when I get to the convenience store purchase of the burner phone. "Do you have the name of the store?"

"No, but Sam probably does."

"I'll check it out. Maybe the storekeeper will remember something about the purchaser; he might even be able to ID Zimmer."

"Good," I say. "Because it will be hard to prove that it was Zimmer's phone, since it wasn't on the truck with him. Why buy it and then throw it away?"

She shakes her head. "Whoever removed the knife removed the phone as well."

I decide not to mention that we haven't demonstrated with any certainty that the knife ever existed. I don't want to start any kind of discord, not with bedtime looming. In the marital sex game, timing is everything.

The wired money, of course, is the most interesting bit of news to Laurie, as it was to me. "Somebody wanted him out of jail and available, and it wasn't to transport dogs," she says.

"You are obviously assuming it was so he would be available to kill Kramer."

"Right, but the significant part is that it was Zimmer. They could have found other people willing to commit a murder for that kind of money, but they wanted Zimmer, even though he was in jail."

I nod. "Because of his history with Kramer."

"Exactly. This is great; we're getting somewhere. I'm happy about this."

"Don't lose that happy mood," I say. "I'll be back soon and will attempt to provide you with even more happiness."

"I'll be in bed reading," she says.

This, in keeping with the theme of the evening, is a mixed bag. The idea that Laurie will be in bed can only be seen as a positive. Her presence is absolutely essential.

But the "reading" part is problematic; sometimes reading makes her fall asleep. I would have preferred she'd said she'd be in bed "waiting," or even better, "yearning."

I take Tara and Sebastian on what I will attempt to make an abbreviated walk. Tara is very cooperative, doing her business within the first five minutes. I think she must be feeling guilty about her traitorous actions with Kramer.

Sebastian is a somewhat different story. He sniffs around endlessly, trying to find the absolute perfect spot. "Sebastian, we have passed at least fifty acceptable trees, signposts, and fire hydrants. Stop sniffing and start pissing, or you have chowed down your last biscuit."

That seems to work; let no man separate Sebastian from his biscuits. We're back in the house about a half hour after we left. I check in on Ricky and kiss his sleeping head. It's a ritual I have started to do every night. One time he even woke up, smiled, and said, "Hi, Dad. I love you."

I don't want to overstate this, but it's a moment I will remember for the rest of my life.

I head for the bedroom, cringing, but Laurie is in fact awake and reading. "You're awake," I say.

"You're very observant. I was waiting for you."

"Were you also yearning?"

"Don't push it," she says.

"What about craving? Lusting? Longing?"

"Andy . . ."

"Okay. But do any of these fit? Hungering? Aching? Wanting?"

She thinks for a moment. "Let's go with *wanting*."

I can't help but grin my stupid grin. "Yes, let's."

Zimmer lived in a small garden apartment in Lynd-hurst.

The sign in front advertises them as long- or short-term rentals and promises that there will not be any credit check conducted. The manager is Oscar Cabrera, and he just shrugs when Laurie and I inform him we are seeking information about Zimmer.

We're sitting in his office, which is just as dumpy as mine but at least has a window air conditioner. It's a bit loud, but effective in this small space. "You related to any of the baseball Cabreras?" I ask.

He frowns. "You think I'd be here if I was?"

"Who are the baseball Cabreras?" Laurie asks.

"At the risk of stating the obvious, they're baseball players named Cabrera. There's a million of them; Cabrera is like Smith in baseball land. There's Miguel, and Melky, and Ramón, and Asdrúbel, and . . ."

She interrupts. "Okay . . . that's plenty. It's possible we might be starting out a bit off the point," she says.

I nod. "Possible." Then, to Cabrera, "How long did Zimmer live here?"

"About four months."

"Did he get many visitors?"

"Nah. You know, the police already asked me this stuff."

"I'm sure they did," I say. "Bless them for their thoroughness."

"No family that he mentioned?" Laurie asks.

"We didn't spend much time together, you know? If he had a problem in the apartment, he called me. That was it."

73

"Do you know what he did for a living?"

"I know he paid his rent."

We ask him more questions and get similarly nonresponsive answers. I don't think the guy is hiding anything; I just have a hunch he doesn't take much of a personal, caring interest in his tenants.

Finally, Laurie asks, "Do you have any idea where we might find other people who knew him?"

"You could try that bar."

"Which bar is that?" I ask.

"It's called the Cave. I saw him in there once, but I think he went there a lot. He even had a T-shirt from there that he wore all the time."

"Where is it?"

"Downtown. On your right as you drive in."

As we're leaving, I say, "You really should check your family tree. With all those Cabreras, you've got to be related to at least one of them. Even if it's only a third cousin."

"Hey, man. I've checked it out a hundred times, you know?"

We get in the car, and I say, "To the Cave?"

She nods. "To the Cave."

The Cave proves to be a normal dive bar in every respect except for fake stones on the walls, designed to give a cave effect. Instead, it gives a fake stone effect.

There are only four patrons in the bar, although since it's barely 11:00 A.M., it could certainly be argued that the word *only* doesn't apply. Four is a lot for this hour, even though in this case they represent a pretty scraggly group. My guess is that none of them are going to be heading back to their corner offices after a quick lunch.

We walk over to the bartender, who is not surprisingly behind the bar. He's about fifty and looks like he has spent most of his fifty years behind bars just like this.

"Hi, I'm Andy, and this is Laurie."

He doesn't say anything, just eyes us warily.

I smile and say, "This is the part where you introduce yourself, and we all lie and say how nice it is to meet each other."

"What do you want?" is his response.

"To talk about Kenny Zimmer."

"You cops?"

"No."

"He's dead."

"He is?" I ask, feigning shock. "Then I guess he's not coming to the reunion. We were here to ask if he wanted the chicken or the fish."

Laurie rolls her eyes—a sure sign she's about to take over the questioning. "We want to know if he had any close friends that might give us some insight into the reasons he was killed."

"What's it to you?"

"We're friends of the court," I say.

"You're on the side of the killer?"

"We're trying to find out who the killer is," she parries. "Look, there's no reason to make this difficult. We could ask you these same questions in court in a deposition, but why go to all that trouble?"

He thinks about this for a few moments. He's smart enough to know this is a better setting to answer the questions than in court, but not smart enough to know we could never get him into court to answer these questions.

"He's got four buddies; they're here every night."

"What time do they get here?"

"Nine o'clock."

"How will I know them?"

"You don't want to know them, especially when they find out you're on the killer's side. Zimmer was one of them."

"Do they have a regular table?" I ask.

He points. "In the corner." Then he indicates Laurie. "But definitely don't bring her. Come to think of it, don't bring you either. These are not people you want to interrupt."

"Is it a book club or something?" I ask. "Because I just finished a terrific Jane Austen novel I think they might like."

He just shakes his head. "I'm glad I'm off tonight. There's gonna be a lot of cleaning up to do. And I'll tell the night guy to put away the good glasses."

My meeting with Carla Westrum is going to be a short one.

She called and invited me in to discuss the case. She's going to be asking whether we are interested in pleading it out, which we are not. I would have said we should handle our business in a phone call, but there's always the possibility that I'll learn something in the meeting.

Besides, it's not like I have any hot leads to track down. At least not until 9:00 tonight.

In my experience, I have found that prosecutors usually make us defense attorneys wait in the lobby for a while. It's their way of demonstrating that they have the upper hand in the relationship. The annoying part about that is not the waiting; it's the knowledge that they do have the upper hand. They have the resources of the state.

But Carla proves to be the exception to the rule; she's out in the lobby within a minute of the time I arrive to lead me back to her office. Not only that, but she's smiling the entire time, which by itself could get her drummed out of the prosecutors' union.

Once we're settled in her office and I've declined her offer of something to drink, she says, "So you planning to take this to trial?"

"Don't you want to chitchat first?" I ask.

"Business first. Always."

I nod. "Then yes, we're taking this to trial."

"Really? I'm surprised," she says.

"I am full of surprises."

"I was prepared to make you an attractive offer," she says. "Thirty to life, with the possibility of parole after twenty-five."

I put on my most stunned look. "Wow, that's fantastic. I wish I were the wrongly accused so I could take advantage of that myself."

Her smile becomes a laugh. "Wrongly accused? We've got Kramer on video entering the truck, and his gun is the murder weapon. And if we needed motive, which we don't, we have him threatening the life of the victim."

"Sounds airtight to me," I say. "You can consider the defense totally intimidated."

Now her expression is bemused, leading me to believe the prosecution is not quite intimidated. "What is your defense?"

"Innocence, purity, and goodness."

Another laugh. "I'm just glad I'll be there the day you argue that to the jury."

"Good. It will give you something to look forward to. Are we done here?"

"I'll take one more shot at this. Andy, I don't need or want this to pad my résumé, and the state doesn't need the expense of a trial. If you want to talk to your client about this, you've got forty-eight hours. But I can only make this offer once."

"Carla, I rejected it thirty seconds ago. So technically, you're already making the offer twice."

She smiles. "Then yes, we're done here. And just so you'll know, I lied about not wanting to pad my résumé. This will fit in very nicely. So now we can get to the chitchat. How long have you and Laurie been together?"

"Married three years, together for seven."

"Laurie is wonderful," she says.

"I am keenly aware of that."

"You must have something going for you that isn't readily apparent," she says. "I mean, besides the wiseass attitude."

"I'm an onion. One has to peel me one layer at a time."

"I hear you're a good lawyer."

"Stop . . . I promised myself I wouldn't cry."

The meeting was a waste of time in terms of learning more about the prosecution's case. I already knew what she recounted, and that's either because she was too smart to say more or because that's all she has.

But the fact of the matter is that right now they have more than enough and plenty to convince a jury. Even though I am quite sure that Kramer will not take her offer, I do feel an obligation to relay it, and I can't even say he'd be wrong to take it. The likelihood is that he's going to get worse at trial.

At this point, we basically have no defense, which is not a really good position for the defense to be in. The truth, or at least the truth as our client presents it, is that he was acting in self-defense, that Zimmer lured him there to kill him.

But so far, we truly have no evidence of that to point to. What evidence there is shows that Zimmer had no weapon except his bare hands, and no one would believe that he would reasonably use that approach to kill Kramer, especially since Kramer had previously demonstrated an ability to dominate Zimmer physically.

The only thing I can think of, and it's just grasping at straws, is that there was someone else on the truck who took the weapon. But at this point I wouldn't dare tell that to the jury, because the video camera footage doesn't back me up.

So my efforts thus far have been to show Zimmer to be a bad guy, capable of doing the luring and killing. But even if I can show that, even if I could somehow present testimony that Zimmer wanted Kramer dead, I still cannot demonstrate our version of what happened on that truck.

I have to trust Kramer's version, whether I fully believe it or not. So I need to focus on Zimmer's motive. He waited a long time to get his revenge. If he was self-motivated, then we're in trouble. If someone else put him up to it, maybe the third person on the truck, then we have a shot. Especially if that third person is the source of Zimmer's sudden receipt of $75,000.

But we need to know who and why.

G etting put in dangerous situations is not why I went to law school. Actually, I can't remember why I went to law school at all. I think it was probably a combination of me following in my father's footsteps and not being able to hit the curveball. So with major-league baseball eliminated as a possibility, I went the father route.

But Nelson Carpenter, my dad, is a perfect example of what I'm talking about. He had a long and very distinguished career as a criminal prosecutor, and I can't ever recall a situation in which he was at risk of physical violence. Yet it seems to happen to me all the time.

Tonight will be an excellent example. I'll be going to the bar where Zimmer had hung out to talk to his buddies. The bartender described the potential meeting in a rather ominous fashion. I'm a total coward, but on the Carpenter scare-o-meter, it only ranks at about a four out of ten.

I'm just going to ask a few questions, and though they might be enough to annoy the Gang of Four, I won't press it that much. And the important thing is that the meeting will convene in a public place, from which I could back out at a time of my choosing. Backing out is a specialty of mine.

But because there is at least some danger, Laurie and I commence the obligatory pre-danger conference. Laurie believes I would have trouble defending myself in a contentious Girl Scout gathering, and while I pretend otherwise, she happens to be right.

So she insists on going with me to the bar. As a former cop, and an investigator licensed to carry a firearm, she can easily handle the situation. As a lawyer licensed to carry a briefcase, we both know I would be less effective.

But since I also spend time pretending to be a real man, I refuse to put her in danger. "I can deal with this," I say.

"Really?" she asks. "When did you develop that capability?"

"There's a whole side of me you don't know. A fearless, throw-caution-to-the-wind side."

"You don't like wind. It messes up your hair."

I nod. "Right. But I deal with it, because of the fearless thing. Besides, you can't go with me to beat up four hoods in a bar; we don't have a babysitter."

"You're not going alone."

Thus we have gotten to the same place we always get in these arguments. It's a decision that eases her mind and also indulges my pathetic need to not depend on a woman.

We say it at the same time.

"Marcus."

The bartender said that Zimmer's friends arrive at nine o'clock, so I want to get there within ten minutes after that. There's no reason to give them time to drink and get a buzz; the soberer they are, the less likely they are to mess with Marcus.

The way we usually work situations like this is Marcus picks me up and we drive to the meeting place. Marcus then goes in with me and intervenes if I need intervening. But his very presence sets an intervention-discouraging tone.

I have decided to play this one a little differently, mainly because I'm not that worried. Marcus is going to arrive at eight thirty and take a seat at the bar. Then he'll call me when the group arrives, and I'll show up a few minutes later.

Without them knowing that Marcus is with me, the conversation might go more smoothly, and I might learn more of whatever there is to learn. If it doesn't go smoothly, Marcus will be there.

Laurie hugs me when I leave; she does it more intensely than if I were going to mail a letter. I think she probably assumes I can come back from a mailbox relatively intact.

I park about four blocks from the bar and wait for Marcus's call. It comes at nine o'clock sharp; Zimmer's pals are obviously prompt creatures of habit.

Just like every time I face possible danger, my instinct is to turn around and go home, but I overcome it and drive to the bar.

I walk in and see that it's more crowded than this morning, but not exactly packed. There are maybe fifteen or so patrons, three of whom are standing at the pool table in one corner. In another corner, hard to miss, are the four guys the bartender spoke about. Three of them are large and tough looking, at least by my standards. The fourth is average size and tough looking.

Marcus sits at the bar, nursing a beer and watching me enter. His seat is about fifteen feet from the table where the guys are sitting. I walk straight toward the table, and as I get close, I grab a chair from an adjacent table and pull it along with me.

"Hey, guys, you mind if I join you for a few minutes?" I say as I sit down.

"You the lawyer working for the guy that killed Zim?" asks one of the large ones. He's also the one closest to my chair.

This question tells me a couple of things. One is that the bartender passed the word to these guys about me and the fact that I'd be here. The other is that Zimmer's friends called him "Zim."

These are the kinds of clues that I need.

"I'm trying to figure out who killed him, and I'm hoping you can help with that."

"You got thirty seconds to get out of here, or tomorrow another lawyer will be trying to figure out who killed you."

"I just have a few questions. If Zimmer was your friend, you should want to find out the truth."

"Now you got ten seconds," the big guy says, even though I don't think twenty seconds had passed since his last warning.

I look toward the bar and say loudly, "Oh, my God, it's Marcus Clark! Marcus, come on over here. I want you to meet my friends."

Marcus is at the table in about two seconds, but he doesn't seem to have rushed. Marcus appears to glide.

"Talk about a coincidence," I say. "Marcus, what are you doing here?"

Marcus just grunts; it sounds like *nfft*.

"Well, that explains it," I say. "Guys, meet Marcus Clark. Marcus, these are Zim's buddies. Guys, Marcus is my buddy."

The big guy says, "Now you and your friend both have five seconds to get the hell out of here."

"I'm confused," I say. "Is that five seconds for each of us, or five total?"

He clearly has timing issues, but doesn't seem inclined to discuss them, because he stands up, no doubt to enforce his threat. I'm not particularly concerned; the closer Marcus is, the braver I get.

Marcus doesn't even seem to move, but he must have, because the man drops back to his seat, and his head moves forward and down to the table. There is a slight thud when it hits, the group hasn't had time to order any food, so there aren't any french fries or chicken wings on the table to cushion the impact.

Nobody else in the place seems to hear the thud or notice what has happened. Marcus must be like a physical ventriloquist; he does things with his body but you can't tell that he moved. At the end of this particular lightning-fast demonstration of his skill, there are still four of Zimmer's friends at the table, but only three are conscious.

The three of them seem stunned into silence, so I jump back in. "So let's get back to the questions, only we should talk softly, so we don't wake up your friend here."

"How did he do that?" The speaker is the guy next to the unconscious one. He didn't see Marcus move either.

"No, I meant let's get back to my questions, not yours. Why did Zimmer call Kramer to set up a meeting?"

The three of them look at each other, then at their unconscious friend, and then at Marcus. Then the new lead speaker says, "We don't know; Zim never mentioned anything about it."

"Had you noticed anything different about him in the weeks before he died? Did he talk about anything unusual? Or act strangely?" I'm floundering here; I know so little that I don't know what to ask.

"He started spending money. Buying drinks for everybody, talking about the stuff he was going to do."

"Where did he get the money?" I ask.

This time the man hesitates; this cooperation thing is not coming naturally to him.

"The answer is really important to Marcus," I say.

"I don't know. He said he made some contacts; that pretty soon he was going to be set up for good. He said he'd introduce us when the time was right."

"Who were the contacts?"

"I told you, I don't know. But just 'cause Zim said it doesn't mean it was true. He could bullshit with the best of them."

A few more questions do not get us any new information; Zimmer may have used these guys as drinking buddies rather than confiding buddies. Marcus and I get up to leave, just as the unconscious guy is starting to stir.

"Tell him it was a pleasure meeting him," I say.

As I am leaving, I hear one of the three buddies ask the others, "Did you see him do that?"

V ictor Andreson was a semi-frequent patron of the Marriott Marquis hotel in Times Square.

He visited almost every time he was in New York on business, which was probably eight or ten times a year.

Victor didn't stay there as a guest. It was a perfectly fine hotel, but he was used to much more elite accommodations. Victor came to this hotel for a very specific reason.

He used a very upscale escort service, and they took a room that he reimbursed them for as part of the overall cost. It was always a suite, because even as a visitor, Victor had certain standards.

Victor chose the hotel, because while he wasn't a huge celebrity, he had been featured in many business publications and had done quite a few television interviews over the years. The chance of being recognized was slim, but in a huge place like this hotel, he could more easily achieve anonymity.

It was always the same room, 1431, but rarely the same woman waiting there for him. Victor wanted it that way, and the service had never provided anyone that left him disappointed.

He never wanted to stop at the desk to get a key, because he wanted to avoid all personal contact. It reduced the chance of someone realizing who he was. So he went up to the fourteenth floor and knocked on the door.

Today, it was a woman who gave her name as Nancy who opened it. He had no idea if that was her real name, and it was of no consequence to him either way. All he cared about was that she was beautiful, and she certainly was, and that she was talented, and she proceeded to demonstrate that once the door was closed.

Victor had no interest in staying around after they were done. He never did, but in this case, he was running late for a dinner meeting, so he made an even quicker getaway than usual. He gave Nancy three hundred-dollar bills as a tip for a job well done and never expected to see her again.

Once Manning saw Victor leave the hotel, he went up to the fourteenth floor and knocked on the door. Nancy opened it to let him in; she was expecting him.

"How did it go?" he asked.

"Fine. Seemed like a nice guy."

He laughed. "Yeah, he's terrific. But his life is about to take a turn for the worse. You got his prints?"

"All over the room. Should even be some on those hundreds." She pointed to the bills he had left on the night table. She then realized she shouldn't have mentioned that but tried, "Can I keep them?"

"There's others where those came from. We already agreed on a price."

She smiled; the price they agreed on was more than all she had made in the past year.

"So now I make the call?"

"No," Manning said and then turned and slapped her hard across the face, drawing blood. Then he did it twice more, examined his work, and did it twice more again. It left her cowering in the corner of the room, crying.

"You didn't have to hit me so hard," she said through her sobs.

"I'll do what I want when I want," Manning said. "You need to be more grateful; you're making a lot of money. And you know what? There are some people that don't give a damn about you. I am the only reason you will stay alive. You understand?"

Nancy didn't answer, so Manning repeated, with more of an edge in his voice, "You understand?"

"Yes."

"Good. Now you make the call," he said. "You remember the number? It's 911."

Kenny Zimmer apparently waited two years after his assault by Kramer to attempt revenge.

I doubt that he believed in the "revenge is a dish best served cold" theory, so there has to be another reason for the delay. And another reason beyond revenge.

That reason clearly must be money. Suddenly Zimmer got a benefactor who gave him seventy-five grand and maybe promised more in the future. I believe that the sudden influx of money, and the sudden desire to contact Kramer and get revenge, are without question related.

The seventy-five would make a nice down payment on a hit, and I don't see what else Kenny had to offer that would be of similar value. This theory also fits in neatly with the "third person on the truck" assumption.

We are going to be forced into a self-defense approach at trial. Not only is it the truth, but we have to justify Kramer's actions in the moment. Regardless of the background between Kramer and Zimmer, and regardless of Zimmer's reason for wanting him on that truck, we have to get the jury to believe that Kramer did not simply take out his gun and shoot an unarmed man.

But Carla is right; based on the available evidence, the case is a slam dunk for the prosecution. So we have to demonstrate at the very least that Zimmer wanted Kramer dead when he lured him onto that truck. And we have to further show at least the viability that there was a third person there, a person who could have removed the weapon and would have had a reason to.

We have been looking at Zimmer's life, and we must continue to do so, but that is not where the ultimate answer can be found. The answer is in Kramer's life, because Kramer is the straw that stirred this drink. Kramer is the one who someone wanted out of the picture; Zimmer was simply the vehicle sent to make it happen.

I had asked Kramer to prepare three lists. One should include all his current clients, one his less recent clients, and the other anyone who might have enough of a grudge against him to want him dead. None of the information about the relationship between him and his clients would be privileged, because Kramer is an investigator, not an attorney.

Hike is down at the jail getting the lists from Kramer, which gives me some time to go down to the foundation and see how things are going with the new dogs. I had asked Sondra to check with rescue groups in New England to learn if they had been expecting any dogs from this collection, and she tells me that she's finished doing so.

"None of the groups or shelters know anything about these dogs, Andy. I'm not sure where he was going with them."

"Have any of them offered to take any?"

"A few, but not really enough to make it worthwhile. Willie thinks we should place them ourselves; you know how he gets. But this time I agree."

I do know how Willie gets, and I'm not surprised he's made this decision. Once we get dogs, Willie sees them as being under his protection, and he wants to be in charge of which families they go to. It's an attitude and approach that I admire.

"Fine with me," I say.

"Good. We should be ready to get started in about a week."

Willie and Sondra like to get to know a dog before they adopt him or her out. They want to make sure each dog gets with the right family, and for that, they need to know the personalities.

I bring Tara with me because she loves to meet and play with new friends. I don't bring Sebastian because he is asleep and snoring. When Sebastian is sleeping so soundly that he snores, it would take a marching band armed with Tasers to shake him awake.

It may sound weird, but I always find it somehow refreshing to spend time at the foundation. It's a hopeful place, in that all the inhabitants are about to start a new life, with a great attitude and wagging tails. I like being a part of that.

By the time I get home, Hike is there with the lists, and Laurie is already looking at them. I join in and catch up quickly.

The least promising part of the lists, at a quick glance, are those that Kramer feels might have a grudge against him. Many of them are from years ago, when he worked as a cop. A lesser number are not current, which raises the same issue as the one with Zimmer . . . why would they have waited?

But each one has to be investigated because the one we don't examine will be the guilty party. We divide the groups up; some go to me, and others to Laurie and Marcus. All of them will also go to Sam Willis, to dig up whatever background material he can through his online exploits.

We've got a huge hill to climb, but at least we have identified the hill.

That's a start.

Since every name and case will be investigated, there's no compelling reason to prioritize.

So we're going to put our heads down, go down the lists, and check out each item, one at a time. There's no sense having a bias about what might be important until we know more about them all.

That's why I'm sitting in the office of Carol Kvangnes, the head of HR for a midsize office products manufacturer called Scandrick's Office Supplies. Her company employed Kramer on a worker's compensation case, and he listed her as the contact.

Scandrick's takes up two floors of a six-story office building in Elizabeth. The offices are unimpressive and the furniture fairly nondescript; it's my guess they don't use this location as a showroom.

Kvangnes is in her early thirties and has a knowing sort of expression on her face that announces bullshitting is unlikely to have any chance of working on her.

"So you manufacture office furniture?" I ask. "Because I don't see any manufacturing going on here."

"This is just where the back-office stuff is done. If you want to see our manufacturing plant, you go out the front gate, make a left, and go seven thousand miles."

"Asia?"

She nods. "Generally. Thailand specifically."

"Let's talk about Dave Kramer."

"Terrible about what happened," she says. "I don't believe it for a second."

"You know him well?" I ask.

"Not really; talked to him maybe half a dozen times."

"So why don't you believe it for a second?"

She shrugs. "Yeah, maybe he did it." And then she laughs one of those great laughs that makes you want to say funny things to prompt another.

"He was working on a job for you?"

"Right, checking a workers' comp claim."

"But not a manufacturing accident, because that's in Asia generally and Thailand specifically," I say.

"Right. This was a loading dock accident at our warehouse in Cranford. Our employee, Ralph Witherspoon, slipped and fell while loading a tractor trailer. Or so the story goes."

"So why did you need Kramer?"

"We had reason to believe that Mr. Witherspoon might be exaggerating his injury, for the purpose of staying on disability for the next two thousand years."

"What was the injury?"

"Hard to tell. The claim was a spinal injury, which left him confined to a wheelchair."

"And Kramer checked him out?"

"He did and reported back in detail. Even took pictures." She reaches into a folder and shows me a photograph. "Here's one of Mr. Witherspoon leading his bowling team to victory four weeks after the accident. Shot a 227. It made us all proud."

"Mr. Witherspoon is no longer on disability?"

She smiles. "And no longer employed. He might be on the professional bowlers' tour even as we speak."

"So he might hold a grudge against Kramer?"

"Unlikely. I wouldn't imagine Kramer introduced himself; it's not like he told him to pose for this shot. He's a pro, and Witherspoon is obviously a dope. I doubt he knows Kramer exists."

"Maybe someone could have told him about Kramer? Somebody in your office?"

She shakes her head. "No chance. I'm the only one who had that information, and I didn't share it. Secrecy is important. If Witherspoon found out, he would have changed his behavior. I would imagine he likes disability payments even more than bowling."

T he next stop on my "Dave Kramer, This Is Your Life" tour is Englewood.

Brian Collier owns a deli on Grand Avenue, which he cleverly named Collier's Deli. It's been there for as long as I can remember, and though Brian has always been behind the counter when I've been there, the extent of my conversation with him has gone no further than to request he give me the leanest corned beef he has.

He seemed eager to talk to me when I said I wanted to discuss his employment of Dave Kramer. Collier's son, Nick, has been missing for a number of months, and he recently hired Kramer to try to find him.

When I walk in the door, Brian immediately waves and tells his coworker to man the counter. It's a Tuesday morning, so the place is not exactly jumping, though there are two customers being served.

"Come on back in the office," he says, so I walk behind the counter and follow him through a door. He asks me if I want something to drink, and though I usually say no in situations like this, I am in a deli. So I request a Dr. Brown's Diet Cream Soda, which is at the absolute top of the soda scale.

"That's really something about Kramer, huh?"

I nod. "Really something."

"I never would have guessed it," he says, then shakes his head in amazement in order to demonstrate physically his verbally expressed inability to have ever guessed it.

"Tell me about your son," I say. "Please."

"Nick is a good kid; he just went down the wrong path. You know, I think life is a series of choices. You can take two kids, they can be identical in every way, but they make choices as they go along. And sometimes they are dumb choices, and sometimes they don't even know they're making them." He shakes his head sadly. "But once you make them, you're stuck with them. And they're part of you forever."

"What was Nick's choice?"

"Drugs. But the thing about drugs is it stops becoming a choice."

The look on his face reflects a pain so deep it can never be dug out, no matter what ultimately happens. It hurts to watch, and as a father it scares the ever-loving shit out of me.

"So Nick ran off?" I ask.

He nods. "Four times. The first three times he came back; this time he didn't. Yet. So I hired Kramer to find him."

"How did you hear about him?"

"I've got a friend who's a state cop; he recommended him."

"Did he have any luck?" Kramer's list does not specify his actions in the case, so I doubt it.

"I don't know; he hadn't reported back to me yet when this happened. I was hoping you were here to maybe give me some information."

"I wish I had some, but I don't. You might want to hire someone else," I say. "Even in a best case, Kramer won't be available for a while."

"You know anyone?"

I nod. "I can send you some names."

"My wife . . . his mother . . . thinks that it's a mistake, that if Nick wants to come back, he'll come back. And if he doesn't, he won't, no matter if we find him or not."

I think she's right, but I don't want to tell him that, because it's none of my business. "I hope he comes back," I say.

As I'm leaving the deli, I look at my cell phone and see that Pete Stanton has called me. His voice mail tells me to call him back, which I do. Before I even ask him what he wanted, I ask if he's familiar with the Nick Collier missing persons case.

"I don't think so," he says. "Wait a minute, is that the son of the guy who owns the deli?"

"Right."

"It's not a missing persons case," he says. "He's a twenty-one-year-old adult who decided to leave. Adults have that right."

I know he's correct, so I don't push it. "You called?"

"Yeah. I'm giving you the chance to invite me to lunch."

"Why would I do that?"

"Because I'm a good conversationalist, and because this is a conversation you will be very interested in."

I'm already interested in it, so we make arrangements to meet at Charlie's in an hour. When I get there, Pete is already at our table. It's disorienting to see him in this place without a beer in front of him, but he doesn't drink on duty.

I no sooner get "hey, Pete" out of my mouth than he sets the ground rules for our conversation. "Who's buying lunch?" he asks.

"I thought we'd flip for it."

"Think again," he says.

"Okay. I'm buying."

"And who's paying for burgers and beer for the rest of the natural life of Pete Stanton and Vince Sanders?"

"Now you're doing Vince's dirty work?"

"He's a personal friend of mine." Then he adds, pointedly, "What's mine is his. So if I have permanent access to your money, then he has permanent access to your money."

"Heartwarming. Okay, I'm buying. It's not like that changes anything."

"And these generous gestures have nothing to do with our upcoming conversation?"

"Can we get to the upcoming conversation?" I ask. "Because at this rate I'm going to be buying dinner."

"Answer the question."

"Right. The generous gestures are from the pure goodness of my heart. There is no bribery involved."

"Glad we cleared that up. Let's order, and then we'll talk."

We got prints from the storage rooms in the truck," Pete says.

As conversational starters go, this is a really good one. I don't ask whose prints they are, because obviously that's what Pete is here to tell me, so there's no sense delaying things.

"There were prints from six different people, so we ran them all through the database. We found matches for five of them. Three were military with no criminal record. One had a conviction for passing bad checks, and the fifth is the reason we're having lunch."

"I'm all ears," I say.

"Good for you. His name is Eric Benjamin. You ever hear of him?"

"No. I don't think so," I say.

"He was a state cop, until about six years ago. Big shot detective, star on the rise."

"You said *was* a state cop."

He nods. "You're a good listener. Internal Affairs went after him; he was accused of beating up a potential suspect in an investigation, but more importantly, he was accused of confiscating certain criminal property for his own personal gain."

"Drugs?"

Pete nods. "And money. It was believed that when Benjamin made a number of arrests, valuable evidence and property never actually made it to state custody."

"What happened to him?"

"Not much. His main accuser was a guy by the name of Orlando

Guadalupe. But before actual charges could be brought, most of Mr. Guadalupe's body was found in an alley in Garfield."

"Most?"

"Right. His arms were found in an alley in Lyndhurst, and his head was found in another alley in East Rutherford."

"So without Guadalupe, there was no case?"

"Depends on who you talk to. People in the department certainly thought there was, but the state attorney turned chickenshit. He was afraid they didn't have enough, and he didn't want to bring a case like that, which was sure to generate a lot of publicity, and then possibly lose it. Might impact his political ambitions."

"Where is Benjamin now?" I ask.

"I have no idea, but it's a pretty good bet he hasn't entered the priesthood."

"Do you know why he was on that truck?"

"No idea. And did I give you the impression I was conducting the investigation for you?"

"Which brings me to the obvious question. Why are you telling me all this? If you gave it to Carla, I would have gotten it in discovery."

"You are the one who asked me to get the prints. So I wanted to make sure you got them."

"You think Carla would have withheld this?"

"I don't know her, but I don't trust lawyers no matter what side they're on. They are among the lowest life-forms we have."

"Stop, you're making me blush."

"And whatever you do, don't turn this into me thinking your boy is innocent, because I don't, and he isn't."

"Right," I say. "Eric Benjamin was on the truck because he was adopting a Pomeranian."

I'm not sure how much to say to Pete. On the one hand, in the world that is our justice system, he is the opposition. On the other hand, I really do believe that he wants to know the truth and does not want anyone to be wrongly convicted even if he is the one who made the arrest. The fact that he is sitting here and telling me about the prints is evidence of that.

"Let me tell you something," I say. "And let me preface it with the fact that if you reveal this to anyone, all previous agreements regarding beer and hamburgers are null and void."

"Here it comes," he says, preparing to mock me.

"Our position is that Kramer acted in self-defense, that Zimmer came at him swinging a large knife."

"And Kramer took the knife with him when he left?" he asks. "As a souvenir?"

"No."

"So Zimmer used an invisible knife?"

"No, there was a third person on that truck. After Kramer left, he took off with the knife."

"And since there was a videotape of the entire event, the third person must have also been invisible, so when he left with the invisible knife, the camera couldn't see it." He smacks the table. "That's it! You've cracked the case!"

"If I had that invisible knife with me now, I'd cut out your larynx."

His laugh causes me to believe he doesn't consider me a physical threat. Then he asks the same question that I asked him, "So why are you telling me all this?"

"Because if you know what really happened, you might be more inclined to realize it if you learn something that confirms it. I'm trying to compensate for your lack of smarts, which requires a great deal of compensation."

"Hearing that causes me to want a beer," he says, signaling to a waiter.

"You're on duty," I point out.

"Right you are. I'm getting a couple of six packs to go. Is your tab paid up? I don't want to be embarrassed."

Sam, it might be time to break out the Bubalah Brigade."

Bubalah is the pet name for Sam given him by one Hilda Mandlebaum, who along with her husband, Eli, and friends Morris Fishman and Leon Goldberg, took a seniors' computer class that Sam gave at the YMHA.

Despite the fact that they have logged at least 330 years between them, they were attentive, eager learners. Sam was amazed at their attitude and proficiency, and we have actually used them to help on a couple of cases. They have proven invaluable.

"Really?" Sam asks. "Because I can handle what we have so far."

"We're adding a lot," I say. "Besides, I could go for some more of Hilda's rugelach." If I were condemned to death, Hilda's rugelach would account for my last ten meals.

"Okay, I'll call Hilda, and she'll round up the team. What have you got?"

I tell him all that I know about Eric Benjamin, though I don't bother going into the fact that his fingerprints were found in the truck. Knowing or not knowing that will in no way impact what Sam is doing.

"I want to know as much as you can find out about him," I say, "including how I can reach him if I choose to."

"That's it?" he asks.

"No. I then need you to cross-check him with every name on Kramer's list, regardless of their reason for being on the lists. I want to know if there are any connections between Benjamin and any of them. Including phone calls."

"I'll call Hilda right away," he says, no doubt realizing the enormity of the assignment.

I have an appointment in an hour to check out the next name on Kramer's list, so that gives me time to call Laurie and tell her what I've learned. She has heard of Benjamin; as an ex-cop, she pays special attention to media stories about cops gone bad. It's accurate to say that they are not her favorite people.

She's also excited about what the presence of Benjamin's prints in the truck might mean. I'm not quite as optimistic about it as she is, but I'm not as optimistic about anything as she is. I'm not Hike, but I'm also not Mr. Sunshine.

My next phone call is to George Davenport, the owner of the dog transport truck and Kenny Zimmer's final employer. "Does the name Eric Benjamin mean anything to you?" I ask.

"No. Should it?"

"He's been reported as having been on the truck that Zimmer was driving."

"Afraid I can't help you. For all I know, Zimmer could have had the goddamn Russian army on there. I can't keep tabs on my drivers like that; I just trust that they'll get to where they're going."

"Have you done any checking to find out where the dogs were going? Because we haven't had any luck doing that." I ask because it's been bugging me that there was no one waiting for these dogs. If Zimmer had nowhere to take them, what the hell were they doing on the truck in the first place? He didn't have anyone on the other end to pay for them.

"Why would I bother checking?" Davenport asks. "I don't have the dogs, remember?"

With that ultra-helpful conversation behind me, my next stop is in Short Hills to meet with Christine Craddock, one of Kramer's more recent clients. I hope he was charging her a healthy fee, because based on this house, she can afford it.

Short Hills is one of the more exclusive areas of New Jersey, and Ms. Craddock lives in one of the more exclusive parts of Short Hills. Not surprisingly, I am greeted at the door by a butler type. I'm dressed in jeans and a pullover shirt, and he looks at me like I am the hired help, the irony being he is actually the hired help.

"Mrs. Craddock is expecting you," he says.

I nod. "And I am expecting Mrs. Craddock."

I'm led to a room that appears to be a library, since the walls are primarily made up of bookshelves filled with books. The only reason I hesitate to call it a library is because it doesn't have those cabinets with Dewey decimal file cards or newspapers on those wooden sticks.

After a few minutes, the door opens and Mrs. Craddock comes in. She is surprising to me in a couple of ways. First, she's younger than I'd expected; the house is furnished in a conservative, old-money kind of way. But Mrs. Craddock can't be more than thirty-five, with a terrific, welcoming smile.

The next thwarter of Carpenter expectations is the fact that Mrs. Craddock is in a wheelchair. It gives me a wave of guilt; despite my own wealth, I've caught myself begrudging her obvious privilege. The fact of the matter is she is clearly not skating through life on a wave of unending good luck.

"Mr. Carpenter, I'm glad you're here," she says.

"Really? I don't get that kind of a welcome very much."

She smiles warmly. "I find that hard to believe. You're representing Dave Kramer?"

She asks the question even though I told her I was when I spoke to her on the phone. "Yes. He did some work for you?"

"He did; two separate assignments."

"Can I ask in what capacity?" I basically know the answer from Kramer's lists, but I like the person I'm interviewing to give me as much information as possible. Sometimes it reaffirms what I know, and sometimes not.

"It's somewhat embarrassing, but I asked him to confirm for me that my husband was having extramarital affairs; I guess *cheating* is the word you would use."

I know from Kramer's notes that her husband was some kind of big shot in the computer industry, but I'd never heard of him. "You use the word *confirm*," I say. "You had reason to believe it was the case, but you wanted to know for sure?"

"Yes, something like that. And Kramer validated my suspicion in a matter of a couple of days. He was quite good at his job, and I must say quite sensitive in how he conveyed his findings to me. He said he had photographic evidence, but I declined to see it."

"That must have been upsetting," I say.

"Yes, but not for the reasons you might imagine. Since my accident, I am simply not the person I was, nor could I be the wife I was. I had no problem with John seeing other women; they were not a substitute for me. He still loved me, which is really all I cared about."

"So why were you upset?"

"Because he wasn't honest with me about it. Honesty was something we always promised each other, and I regretted that betrayal."

"You said you employed Kramer for two assignments. What was the other one?" I ask the question knowing the answer, and not looking forward to hearing it.

"John passed away almost three months ago."

"I'm sorry."

"Thank you. He was hiking in the mountains and slipped and fell to his death. That's what they said."

"You don't believe that?"

"No. John loved being out in the natural world. He craved it; we shared that before my accident. But he also had great respect for that world; he understood the dangers and was totally careful. He would not have put himself in that position; I just don't believe it and never will."

"He was out there alone?"

"Yes. He loved the solitude. He said it cleansed his mind and body."

"Do you know of anyone who might have wanted him dead?"

She shakes her head. "I don't. My suspicion is that it might have to do with his business life. John was brilliant, and that was reflected in his success."

"So you hired Kramer to find out what really happened?"

"Yes."

"Did he?"

"I would doubt it, because he would have told me. But it was very early; I would expect it to take longer."

"What will you do next?"

"I haven't made a final decision, but I suspect I will find someone else to undertake the job. It's difficult in that it's a world I am completely unfamiliar with and rather intimidated by."

"Would you like me to have someone call you who could offer you advice?"

"Certainly, yes."

"I'll do that. Her name is Laurie Collins."

I thank her and leave. I hope she gets her answer, and I hope she can ultimately accept that her nature-loving husband who was so successful did one other stupid thing in his life besides cheating on her.

He got too close to a cliff.

Anthony Orlando is the proprietor of a car wash on Route 17 in Paramus. He's on Kramer's list not as a client but as someone who might have held a grudge against him. If he has a grudge against anyone, it should be his parents, for giving him that name.

He agrees to talk to me in the office of the car wash. He's a big guy, at least 240 pounds, with a weathered face. He might have spent too much time going through the wash himself. I have to admit that if I owned a car wash, I might be tempted at least once to walk through it naked as a way to take a shower.

"I guess you never use 'Tony,' huh?" I ask.

He shakes his head. "Not since I was a kid. I got tired of people asking me where Dawn was, or if I tied a yellow ribbon to the damn oak tree."

"I can sympathize," I say. "A girlfriend in high school named Karen dumped me because she was afraid she'd wind up Karen Carpenter." I leave out the part about her also telling me I was an asshole.

He doesn't seem that interested in my high school dating issues. "So they nailed that scumbag Kramer, huh?"

"He's been arrested and is facing trial."

"Good."

"You don't like him?" I ask.

"What tipped you off?"

"Instinct. Why do you feel that way?"

"I got in a bar fight; I beat the hell out of a guy who deserved getting the hell beat out of him. Kramer showed up with a few other cops and arrested me."

"Wasn't he just doing his job?"

"On the arresting part, yeah. But he tased me when I had already backed off; there was no reason for that. You ever been tased?"

"No. Lawyers try to remain tase-free."

"Well, it is the worst, believe me. You feel like your whole body is going to explode. Did they tase Kramer when they caught him?"

"No."

"Too bad. So what do you want?"

"I'm just trying to track down and talk to people that might have had a grudge against Kramer."

"There will be a lot of them," he says.

"Maybe you can rent a hall and have a reunion."

He laughs. "Yeah, we can all wear name tags, and . . . hey, you think I might have something to do with what's going on with him?" His tone changes as he asks the question; he's starting to see me as more of a threat than a buddy to chat with.

"Somebody set him up," I say. "You swore you would get revenge on him."

"Man, you've got to be kidding. That was three years ago."

"It took a while to plan this."

"Get the hell out of here. I don't have time for this. I got a business to run."

"Can I take that as a denial of involvement?"

"Here's what you can take," he says. "You can take your ass off this property. Because if you don't, a bunch of cops are going to come tase me for kicking that ass."

"Tell me the truth. You ever take a shower in the car wash?"

"Do I need to warn you again?"

No. He doesn't.

There are two possibilities regarding our progress in preparing our case. One, and it seems most likely, is that we're not making any. The other is that we are in fact making progress but don't know it. The difference between the two possibilities simply would relate to the depth of shit that we're in.

But either way, it's deep.

It's possible that someone on Kramer's list is in fact responsible for his current plight, and it's even possible that one of our team has talked to that person. But we certainly haven't identified anyone as a suspect.

Once I've gone through the remainder of my portion of Kramer's list, I call a meeting with Laurie, Marcus, and Hike. We do it at the house; it's ninety-five degrees outside, and air-conditioning is essential.

Hike is the first to arrive.

"How's Darlene?" I ask.

"She's good, Andy. But she went back home. We're going to slow down a little."

"Well, I hope things work out. She seems perfect for you."

"I think so too. But she's nervous. She's not sure I'm ready to settle down; she doesn't think I have a serious side."

"You hide it really well," I say.

He nods his agreement as Laurie and Marcus come into the room. Hike actually backs away slightly; his body language always reveals that he's even more scared of Marcus than I am.

We go through the names on Kramer's list one after the other. Laurie does the talking for both her work and Marcus's, which is a good thing, because Marcus doesn't talk. Although I bet when he was double-dating with Laurie and Kramer, he was a regular raconteur.

She sees two possibilities on her list; one is a guy who Kramer roughed up when called to his house on a domestic violence situation. The guy hit his wife again after Kramer arrived, and Kramer decided he needed to be taught a lesson. He and his partner later claimed that Kramer manhandled him because he was resisting arrest, but that's not how the husband sees it.

The guy has since served time for another assault and has been rather open about his hatred for Kramer.

The other one Laurie considers worth following up on is a drug dealer that Kramer put away for five years. He got out of prison just two months ago and also does not conceal his bitterness. Laurie said that he threatened her for helping Kramer, and Marcus had to convince him that talking that way to Laurie was not a particularly healthy thing to do.

Neither Laurie nor Marcus have any confidence that either of their candidates was involved in the Zimmer killing, and I feel the same way about the only two I have that are even worth mentioning.

One is Anthony Orlando, the tased car wash owner. I just don't buy that after all this time, and after starting and operating a business, that Orlando would suddenly have gone to these lengths to frame Kramer. It also seems a bit subtle; I think if Orlando was set on revenge, he would have taken it more directly.

The other is the case in which Kramer was trying to find out whether John Craddock accidentally fell off the cliff to his death. I lay out the situation, and Hike says, "Kramer was called in afterward just to examine the facts. How could that have anything to do with Zimmer?"

"I don't see how it does," I say. "I'm mentioning it because it includes two factors: potential violence, if Craddock was murdered, and money, because Craddock was a very successful businessman. I'd also like to look into it a bit to give his wife some closure."

I say that I promised Christine Craddock that Laurie would call her to help her plan her next steps, and Laurie says that she will.

Laurie thinks that our best lead so far is the fingerprints of Eric Benjamin that were found on the truck. "We need to find him," she says. "He could have been the third person on the truck."

"On the other hand, he could have been on that truck a year ago, before Davenport even bought it. He was a cop; maybe he stopped the truck to search for illegal cargo and left his print then. Right now, we have no way of knowing when he was on there."

"So we need to connect him to Zimmer," Laurie says.

"Right."

Laurie updates me on a rare piece of good news. "I called the convenience store down in Little Rock where the phone was purchased. I'm sure it was sold to Zimmer."

"How do you know?"

"The owner of the store is a very nice Southern lady named Betty Stuart. I emailed her a photo—I used one of Zimmer's mug shots—and she said she remembers him very well. Said the reason she does is that he pulled into the strip mall with a tractor trailer. Nobody else could get in or out until he left. She said he seemed not to care that he was causing a problem."

"Would she come up and testify?"

"She'd love to."

I'm very pleased by that news. It means we can show that Zimmer called Kramer. It doesn't prove anything, but it sure would have been a lot worse had Kramer initiated the contact.

I tell Hike to go down to the jail and ask Kramer if he knows Benjamin. They were both cops, albeit in different police departments, but they certainly could have run into each other. Maybe they were hated enemies, and Kramer just forgot to put him on the list.

We should be so lucky.

I head down to Sam's office to see how he and his team are doing. As I'm walking through the hot sun to my car, I'm afraid that the Bubalah Brigade is going to collapse in a heap in the un-air-conditioned office. I've got to get them a hotel suite to serve as their base of operations.

But when I arrive there, I am very pleased to feel a burst of cool air as soon as I get in the hallway. And Sam's office is positively cold. I greet the brigade and immediately dive into Hilda's rugelach. Once I'm stuffed, I say to Sam, "So Sofia finally came through and had the AC fixed, huh?"

"Sofia? Eli Mandlebaum fixed it; turns out he was a master electrician."

Eli overhears us talking and says, "No problem; there was a short. Been retired twenty-three years, but electricity is electricity."

Now that that's been settled, I ask Sam how the gang is doing. "They dove right in, Andy. They're amazing."

"When do you think you'll have something for me?"

"Preliminary by tomorrow."

"Please focus hard on Eric Benjamin."

Sam nods. "Hilda's on it. She's like a dog with a bone."

What a complete and total pig," Laurie says.

I'm just entering our bedroom from the bathroom when I hear her say this. My natural assumption is that I just left toothpaste residue in the sink again, a pet peeve of hers, but then I wonder, how could she know that already? There are two possibilities: she has a bathroom sink webcam set up, or she's not talking about me.

"Which pig are we talking about?" I ask, cringing slightly.

She points to the television, which is tuned to *Good Morning America*. On the screen is a photograph of one Victor Andreson, and the chyron at the bottom of the screen says, "Under arrest on multiple charges."

"Who is he?" I ask.

"The head of Victor's Donuts."

"Uh-oh," I say. "We own some of their stock. I hope one of the charges is not doughnut poisoning." Our investments are handled by Edna's broker cousin, Freddie, who has done very well for us. He's knowledgeable and a hard worker, the latter a trait he does not share with his cousin.

I've given Freddie pretty much free rein to buy and sell as he sees fit; very often I don't even know what stocks we own. I only know about Victor's Donuts because Freddie mentioned to me how well we did on it.

"Why would we own his stock?" Laurie asks.

"Because we didn't know he was a bad guy, and he sells a gazillion doughnuts. Not necessarily in that order. By the way, what is he charged with?"

"Soliciting prostitution and then physically assaulting the woman. They showed a picture of her injuries; he beat the hell out of her. Now that we know, I don't think we should be supporting this guy or his company."

"Are we disregarding the 'innocent until proven guilty' concept?"

She nods. "We are."

I stop talking to watch the rest of the piece. They refer to the amazing success story that Victor's Donuts has become and how the stock soared as a result. Andreson was apparently a brilliant businessman, knowing exactly where to place his stores and how to price out the competition.

He was also considered a "doughnut genius," a population subgroup I never realized existed. He created types of doughnuts that were unique and that people went crazy for.

We benefited from all of this; it was one of Cousin Freddie's best moves.

The news anchor mentions that he is claiming to be innocent, but I don't think anyone is taking that too seriously. As evidence of that disbelief, the announcer also says that the stock is down 22 percent in pre-market trading, meaning it's time to call Freddie.

"Hey, Andy," Freddie says when he hears my voice. "Not a good way to start the day."

"I assume you're talking about the doughnut stock?"

"I am," he says. "We're long the stock."

I'm not familiar with that expression. "Obviously 'long' is bad?" I ask. "We'd rather be short?"

"Yes, right now we'd much rather be short."

"Anything we can do? Can we shorten it?"

He laughs, no doubt at my ignorance. "No, we can't shorten it. All I would recommend at this point is waiting for the stock to go back up. The fundamentals are sound, but it's going to be a while; the market will have to believe they can adequately replace this guy. And the worst part is that I'm not sure they can."

"Laurie doesn't approve of investing in a stock run by a guy she affectionately calls a 'complete and total pig.'"

"He won't be running it anymore."

"I know, but she wants nothing to do with him or it."

"This is the wrong time to sell, Andy," he says.

"I should have spoken to you before I married someone with ethics and principles. Find the best time to get out, but let's do it this week."

"You're the boss," he says.

"Mention that to Laurie when you get a chance."

I'm no sooner off the phone than Sam Willis calls.

"Hilda found Eric Benjamin," he says.

"Great. How did she do it?"

"She googled his name."

"I could have done that," I say.

"That's open to question," Sam says, based on his knowledge of my computer skills. "Regardless, don't mention that to Hilda. But it wasn't exactly tough. He'd probably be in the damn phone book, if damn phone books existed anymore. He's not hiding, that's for sure."

"Where is he?"

"He's president and CEO of a company called the EB Group. I think it's fair to say that *EB* stands for Eric Benjamin."

"What do they do?"

"Website says corporate security, but it's notably short of information," Sam says.

"Who are their clients?"

"That's one of the pieces of information that's lacking. I'll attempt to find out through other means."

He gives me the phone number for the EB Group, and I call. I get a computer that asks me to verbalize who I am trying to reach. I inform the computer that I am trying to reach Eric Benjamin, and it puts me on hold. I wait for at least two minutes, but I don't mind, because the computer tells me that my call is very important to them.

Finally, another computer comes on and tells me that Mr. Benjamin is not available and that I am welcome to leave a message. I leave my name and phone number and say that I am an attorney wanting to speak to Mr. Benjamin about a significant matter.

I do not expect to hear back from Mr. Benjamin but would relish another chance to chat with his computer.

I head down to Ricky's room, where he's playing a video game.

Ricky is not devoted to them, at least not as much as I'd have been as a kid in a similar situation. If these options were available to me back then, I would never have left the house.

"You want to have a catch?" I ask. It should be said at this point that in New Jersey you have a "catch" with a baseball, and a "pass" with a football. Getting that wrong would be akin to going to the "beach" rather than to the "shore."

"Sure," he says.

It pleases me to no end that Ricky is always up for doing things; he grabs at life in a way that I never did. "Get your glove," I say.

We go into the backyard and throw the ball around for half an hour. Most of the time is spent with me in a catcher's crouch as Ricky pretends to be the pitcher. His pretending extends to his holding imaginary runners on first base before coming to the plate. He holds them on for a really long time.

"You can throw it anytime you like," I say while my knees are begging me to get up.

"I'm afraid he's going to steal."

"Don't worry; if he tries it, I'll throw him out."

Laurie calls us in for lunch, which is a good thing, since if I have to spend one more minute in the crouch, it will take a crane to get me up. As I'm entering the house, my cell phone rings.

"Carpenter? Eric Benjamin."

"Thanks for calling me back."

"You have questions for me? Let 'er rip."

"I was hoping we could meet. I 'rip' better in person."

"What are you doing for lunch tomorrow?"

He's going to be in Manhattan tomorrow, so we make plans to meet at La Masseria, an Italian restaurant on Forty-eighth Street.

That's just twenty-four hours away, about fifteen miles from here, so based on the normal traffic getting into and out of the city, I probably should leave now.

Do you know Eric Benjamin's cell phone number?" I'm asking Sam the question because it came through on the call to me as "Private Caller" on my caller ID.

"That's insulting to Hilda," Sam says. "She's done a deep dive on him. She has his cell number, home number, address, mortgage, and probably knows the last time he took a piss. Hilda's better at this than she is at rugelach." Sam is clearly proud of his eighty-six-year-old protégé.

"What about his office phone?"

"Doesn't have one; he must work out of his home."

"I'm going to be having lunch with him tomorrow at a restaurant in Manhattan. I want to know who he calls afterward."

"For how long after the lunch?"

"At least for the rest of the day. Even longer if this can be done."

"It's a piece of cake, or rugelach," Sam says. "We can't listen in on the call, you understand. But we can find out who he calls or who calls him. I'll put Leon on this one; he knows his way around the phone company computers better than they do."

"Perfect. That's what I want."

Once I get off with Sam, I consider having Marcus be there tomorrow as well. Not to protect me; unless Benjamin poisons the spaghetti, I should be fine in a Midtown Manhattan restaurant at lunchtime. I could have him follow Benjamin and see where he goes when we're finished, but I decide against it as unnecessary.

Hike comes over with more discovery documents; I'm not spending much time in the office even though it is now cool and comfortable, thanks to Eli Mandlebaum. Sam told me that Sofia Hernandez gave each of the Bubalah Brigade a whole watermelon to thank them for fixing the air-conditioning.

There are quite a few more forensics reports, including the ballistic tests on Kramer's gun. It comes as no surprise that the weapon did fire the shot that killed Zimmer.

The coroner also has certified that Zimmer died of a bullet wound. It's possible she based that on the huge hole in Zimmer's chest.

There is another item that has more significance, at least in terms of how I judge my adversary. They've sent the results of the additional fingerprint testing done on the truck. It is displayed in as unobtrusive a way as possible, buried amid mounds of material. Additionally, the prints are identified without giving the full names of those who left them.

For example, and most importantly, Eric Benjamin becomes E. Benjamin. Had Pete not told me about it, there is a chance that I would not have picked up on it or realized what it meant. I like to think that I would have, but I can't be sure.

There is always the possibility that Carla does not know who Benjamin is; she was in California when his issues with the law and state police came to light. That would be the innocent explanation; the other possibility is that Laurie was right when she described Carla as an ultracompetitive, win-at-all-costs person.

Pete has also gotten me the video that I requested of my last trip to the rest stop. It shows what I wanted it to show, although I'm disturbed by one thing; I'm looking a little paunchy these days. We have a treadmill and exercise bike in our house; it's possible that I actually have to use them for them to be effective.

Hike also brings me a briefcase full of documents regarding the death of John Craddock. It includes police reports on the investigation they conducted, news stories that ran right after the accident, and background information that Sam and his team have accumulated.

Christine Craddock described her husband as successful, which was dramatically understating the case. He was a pioneer in robotics, which is one of the few fields that is so new and developing that there is room for actual pioneers. His company was called Roboton and, based on the information I am reading, it immediately took a position as a leader in the field.

Unlike in more established industries, individuals in nascent fields like robotics can mean everything to a company. General Electric or AT&T can have chief executives that are important to their respective companies, but if they leave, they can be replaced. Maybe the replacement will not be as competent or effective, but the companies will go on and usually thrive.

Not so with companies like Craddock's. It is a highly competitive field; they were competing with other start-ups vying for dominance. Craddock's departure will likely be, if not a death knell for Roboton, a grievous wound.

But while his death might have been a boon to his competitors, there is absolutely nothing here that indicates murder. He was hiking on dangerous terrain and is not the first person to die in that area.

Even taking the opposite view, that he was pushed to his death in a premeditated murder, that's a long stretch from having anything to do with setting up Dave Kramer. But I'll talk to Kramer to see if he can provide any further insight.

That talk will have to wait, because for now I have to read up and learn what I can about Eric Benjamin. It could be an interesting lunch.

L a Masseria is on West Forty-eighth Street near Eighth Avenue.

That puts it in the heart of the theater district, which means it's dependent on Broadway patrons. Like many other nearby restaurants, when it comes to dinner, pre-theater and post-theater hours find it packed. Between 8:00 and 10:00 P.M., however, tables are easy to come by.

Matinees are a similar boon to theater restaurants. They take place on Wednesdays, Saturdays, and Sundays, so at lunchtime on those days, they are always crowded.

Today being Thursday, there are no matinee crowds to contend with. I arrive at the restaurant right at the designated 12:30 time and give the maître d' Benjamin's name. He nods and brings me directly to the table; I get the feeling that Benjamin is a regular here.

Benjamin is waiting for me, and he stands to shake my hand when I reach the table. He's medium height and obviously in great shape; there's a toughness to his face and demeanor that I could easily match with a tough cop working the street. This guy could have been a regular in the cast of one of the four hundred incarnations of *Law and Order*.

Something about him is intimidating. Not Marcus intimidating, but you wouldn't want to run into him in an interrogation room. If he says, "Try the veal; it's the best in the city," I'm out of here. No one has ever confused me with Michael Corleone, and I doubt there's a gun taped to the toilet.

"Good to meet you," I say.

"You don't remember me?"

"No. Have we met?"

"You cross-examined me in a murder case about eight years ago."

I have absolutely no recollection of it; I've cross-examined a lot of cops. It's one of the reasons they hate me, despite my charming and affable personality. "I hope I was gentle," I say.

"Let's just say you're lucky you didn't run into me in the parking lot afterward."

"That's why I take a bus to court."

The waiter comes over and takes our orders. He has a chicken dish, and I get the branzino, once I confirm that they are willing to cut off the head before they bring it to me.

"What's the matter with the head?" Benjamin asks.

"It makes it impossible for me to pretend it was never alive, and the eyes give me the creeps. I don't like to eat anything that can watch me while I'm doing it."

He just shakes his head at my squeamishness. There's also some irony at play here; if the police suspicions are correct, Benjamin would not only cut the head off a branzino, he cut the head off Orlando Guadalupe for squealing on him.

"So ask your questions," he says. "I'm curious."

"Your name has come up in connection with a case I'm working on."

"The Zimmer murder?" When he sees my reaction, he adds, "I checked you out. It wasn't hard; you don't exactly have a lot of clients."

"I go for quality rather than quantity."

"How did my name come up?"

I've decided to be up front with him. If he learns the truth another way, he might have time to come up with a story. If I confront him with it as a surprise, he might be more prone to make an error. In addition, I'll be able to judge his reaction in the moment.

"Zimmer was murdered on a tractor trailer that he was driving."

"So?"

"Your prints were found on the truck."

"Bullshit."

I'm surprised by his reaction for two reasons. First, and most important, he knows that fingerprint evidence is not bullshit. If his prints
are on the truck, then he was on the truck. Everyone knows that, and
he was a cop, so he knows it better than anyone. Even though this was
sprung on him, the fact that he couldn't come up with a better story, or
any story at all, is unexpected.

Of course, "bullshit" could have meant that he thinks I am lying
to him about the print being there. But he's not questioning where I
got the information; he's simply denying it. That doesn't ring true.

The second surprise is his nonverbal reaction. He doesn't seem worried, or flustered, or panicked in any way. He is coldly calm and unfazed.
He told me that my statement was bullshit, and he didn't care if I
believed him or not.

"You're saying you were not on that truck?"

His stare seems to go right through me. "I'm saying two things.
One, I was never on that truck. Two, you'd better be careful who you're
accusing."

Before I can answer, the waiter comes over and places the food down
in front of us. I wait to respond until he leaves.

"I wasn't accusing you of leaving a fingerprint in the truck," I say.
"I was stating a fact, and one the police are aware of. And I'm getting
the feeling that you're threatening me."

"But you're not sure?"

"I'm pretty good at threat detecting, and that sounded like one."

He leans forward, not taking his eyes off of me. I'm not much for
eye contact, but in this case, it feels like I'm left with no choice. "Let
me clear it up for you, counselor, so you can be sure. I was never on that
truck, and I have nothing to do with your case. And if you push it, if
you drag me in, it will be the biggest mistake you have ever made in
your life."

This guy is chilling. I can't put my finger on it, but there is something about him that scares me, right now in the moment, even though
I'm sitting in a crowded, public restaurant. It's more than the words
he is saying, as threatening as they may be. It's his demeanor; there's
a combination of intensity and coldness that is impossible to miss.

But it's suddenly very important to me that I don't back down, even though I've always considered backing down my specialty. "I don't have to drag you in," I say. "You're already in. And that was your biggest mistake."

With that, I stand and walk out of the restaurant. Let him eat my branzino; he's paying for it.

C hesterfield Township sits close to the geographic center of New Jersey.

Being situated in the geographic center of New Jersey is not necessarily everyone's dream, which may explain why less than eight thousand people live in Chesterfield.

Chesterfield is sixty-seven miles from New York City, thirty-five miles from Philadelphia, and one hundred sixty-nine miles from Washington, D.C. It is surrounded by thousands of acres of farmland.

Were you to fire a Soviet-made Iskander-M surface-to-surface missile from Chesterfield, the hypersonic-speed missile would get to Washington in 1.8 minutes. Obviously, because of the closer distance, the time to get to New York and Philadelphia would be less.

This is significant, because in a barn three miles from the center of Chesterfield, there are twenty-three Iskander-M missiles. Ten of them are pointed toward targets in New York, nine toward Washington, D.C., and four toward Philadelphia.

The purchase of the land, and the construction of the barn, were done strictly to house the missiles. The barn has five large doors, to be raised from floor to ceiling, so that the mobile launchpads can roll out, allowing the missiles to be in firing position within minutes.

It has so far taken eighteen months to procure the weapons and ship them safely and undetected to Chesterfield. Rodgers has supervised the entire process, and it is nearing completion. Once that is done, the weapons can be prepared and aimed.

The hard part will be over.

I haven't visited my not-that-tall, not-that-good-looking, unmarried client in a while.

I generally don't like it to go this long, because clients languishing in jail generally want to feel that someone out there is paying attention to them. I don't think Kramer needs as much hand-holding as the typical client, but I'm still stopping there on the way back from my meeting with Benjamin. I also have some questions for him.

But first, of course, he has his questions for me. He asks them in ten different ways, but they basically come down to two. What have you come up with? What are our chances at trial?

My answers come down to not much, and slim. One thing I never do is bullshit a client. It is his or her life that is at stake, not mine. If we lose, the client is going away for the rest of his life, and I'm going home to take Tara for a walk and tuck Ricky into bed.

So I never lie, and I never sugarcoat. Not to a client. Not ever.

With that unpleasantness out of the way, I say, "Tell me about John Craddock."

He seems surprised. "What do you want to know?"

"Was his death accidental?"

"I don't know, but if I had to bet, my money would be on no."

"You think he was murdered?"

"I don't want to overstate this. Let's just say I think there is at least one person out there, maybe more, who knows what really happened."

"His wife said he was alone, that he cleansed himself with nature or some crap like that."

131

He nods. "I know. Nice lady, but she's wrong. Her husband was a slimeball; he was cheating on her long before she went in that wheelchair. That much I learned."

"So you think there was a woman out there with him?"

Another nod. "Tina Bauer."

"You have a name? Tell you what, instead of me asking questions, tell me everything you know about it."

"I don't know that much. I interviewed some people at his office, and one of them knew that name. He said he believed that she was Craddock's current girlfriend. Then there are notes in Craddock's calendar that refer to her."

"Did you speak to her?" I ask.

"I tried to track her down, but she's gone. No trace of her. Just walked out of her apartment and never looked back. It's possible the two things are not connected, but I doubt it. I've got an entire file on it in my house. You can get it yourself."

"I assume the house is locked?"

"Yeah. But I can tell you where I hide the key for when I forget to bring mine."

"Please tell me it's not under the mat."

He laughs. "No, not under the mat. You think Craddock is connected to the Zimmer hit?"

"I don't know. But I believe someone wanted you out of the way and that Zimmer was paid to do it. When he failed, setting you up was plan B."

He nods. "There's a loose brick in the third step, toward the left. Pull it out . . . the key is in there."

Kramer's house is in Teaneck, and I stop there on the way home. It's a ranch house on a quiet cul-de-sac, and I'm surprised by it. It doesn't seem like a place where a single guy would live; it feels like it should have a family with two kids and a swing set.

I find the loose brick on the step, and sure enough there's a key in there. It opens the front door, and I go toward the back of the house, which is where Kramer said his office is.

Just before the office is a den, and when I glance in there, I realize that this is not going to go well. There's a window that's been broken and then opened.

Somebody has been in this house.

Somebody might still be in this house.

So I'm faced with a choice. I can get the hell out of here or head for the office. The odds that the house was broken into just before I arrived, after all this time, are pretty slim. Not so slim that my legs aren't shaking, but slim.

But I continue on to Kramer's office, and I'm not surprised when I see three file cabinets turned over and dumped on the floor. I look through the contents and am again not surprised that there is nothing having to do with the Craddock case.

I take out my cell phone and call Pete Stanton. I tell him that I'm at Kramer's house and that there has been a burglary.

"You can be very annoying," is his sympathetic response.

"Why don't you send people out here who know what they're doing, if you have any," I say. "My client has been robbed. Maybe the crook left fingerprints, or DNA, or a signed confession."

"I'll send some people over. Anything else?"

"Yes, as a matter of fact. Is there an open case anywhere in the state on a woman named Tina Bauer?"

"Why? Did you meet her on match.com?"

I ignore that and tell him it would likely be a missing persons case, but I would appreciate any information he could get for me as to whether or not she has a record.

"Did I mention you were annoying?" he asks.

"I believe you did."

I give him Kramer's address, and he tells me not to leave. Within five minutes, there are two detectives on the scene. I tell them my story, though I do not mention the subject of the file that I was looking for.

I want it on record that Kramer's house was burglarized, because I might want to tell the jury about it. It may not be significant to them, but it is to me. It tells me that Craddock's death is tied to the Zimmer case.

And it tells me that my client has been telling the truth.

Benjamin ate both his entrée and the branzino.

He always appreciated fine food, so he saw no reason to let it go to waste. He also was not one to panic, so the conversation with Carpenter, while worrisome, was just another annoyance to deal with.

It wasn't until he was back in his apartment, two hours later, that he sent the text. It simply said, "Regular time." The response came two minutes later. "I'll be waiting."

So at the designated time, he called the designated number, and the man operating with the name Elway answered on the first ring. As was his custom, Elway did not say hello; he simply waited for Benjamin to say what he had to say.

"I had an interesting lunch today," Benjamin said. "With Kramer's lawyer, Carpenter."

"What was the subject?"

Embarrassing as it was to a professional like Benjamin, he had no choice but to tell the truth. "I left a fingerprint on the truck."

"I thought you were better than that. Very careless."

"That's easy for you to say," Benjamin said, even though he knew it was true. "Your biggest problem is making sure you use enough sunblock."

"If you had the slightest understanding of my role, perhaps you would have more respect for it."

"Speaking of your role, when the hell are you going to get it done?"

"These things take time, Manning." Benjamin knew he used the name Manning to annoy him, since Benjamin had disdain for the ridiculous security measure it represented. These people thought they were pros, but they were amateurs.

On the other hand, they were amateurs who were in the process of making him rich beyond anyone's wildest dreams.

"Well, time may be running out. Carpenter is smart, and the only chance he has to win his case is by tying me to it. So get moving."

"Maybe you should be telling this to Rodgers."

Rodgers was in charge; they both reported in to him. But they were under strict instructions to only make contact in an emergency or if the issue was crucially important, so Benjamin wasn't ready to do that.

"I'm telling it to you," Benjamin said.

An edge came into Elway's voice; he was not intimidated by Benjamin. He was not a man of violence, but he controlled the money, and that's all Benjamin cared about. So, for now at least, Benjamin did not pose a threat. "The plan is for everything to happen at once. Which means we are waiting on you."

"You won't have long to wait."

When I finally leave Kramer's house, my first call is to Sam.

"Sam, there's a woman named Tina Bauer. I'm not sure where she lives, other than it's probably near here. She's said to be in her mid- to late twenties, and she's missing. Find out what you can, please."

"Tina Bauer?" he asks. "I know that name."

"From where?"

"Hold on."

In less than a minute, Sam gets back on the phone. "Benjamin called her twice. It's in his phone records."

This is a huge development; a clear connection between Benjamin and the Craddock death, though I am not comfortable calling it a Craddock murder.

Moments after I hang up, Pete calls me back.

"Tina Bauer's mother reported her missing two months ago. It was followed up on by the state cops, but they think she just took off. The mother said she had a boyfriend, and the detectives assigned think she left voluntarily. Apparently, she and the mother didn't get along very well."

"Where did she live?"

He pauses while he looks it up. "Morlot Avenue in Fair Lawn."

"Thanks," I say. "This is helpful."

"I live for your praise."

"Pete, I think you should open an investigation into Tina Bauer. The state cops may not have considered it important, but they are wrong. Tina Bauer is either a conspirator in a murder, or a murder victim herself, or both."

"You want to tell me the factual basis for what you just said?"

"I don't. But there is one, believe me. And if she's still alive, she may need help. Or capturing. But either way, it's worth looking into. She is not an adult runaway. I am certain of that."

"Okay," Pete says. "But if you get more information, I want it."

I call Sam back and give him the Fair Lawn home information, which will make his job of checking out Tina Bauer much easier. I also ask him if he has any information yet on calls Benjamin might have made after our lunch. He says he doesn't but expects to fairly soon.

When I get home, I update Laurie on Tina Bauer and the robbery at Kramer's house. For her, it is further but unnecessary confirmation that Kramer is, in fact, innocent.

We're had reversed roles all along on this case. As a defense attorney, I'm usually skeptical of the government's positions, but as a former cop, she has a tendency to assume that arrests are almost always made for good reason.

In this case, she has believed Kramer all along, no doubt because of how well she knows him. I've been the skeptic, probably because I'm harboring this childish jealousy. But it's not like I've ever claimed to be an emotional adult.

For the first time, I feel like we might be getting somewhere in our investigation. The sudden influx of cash into Zimmer's account, the presence of Benjamin's fingerprint on the truck, Tina Bauer's disappearance, and the burglary of Kramer's house . . . all of this leads me to believe we are on the right track.

But we have a trial date barreling down on us, and I've never run into a jury that has bought into the "trust us, we're on the right track" argument, no matter how charmingly I present it.

One thing I haven't focused on to any degree is why John Craddock was murdered, if indeed he was. This was not a wronged girlfriend getting revenge against the lover that jilted her. Benjamin's connection to her would seem to eliminate that as a possibility.

Tina Bauer's role is unclear, at least to me. She could be the killer, or she could have helped Benjamin by luring Craddock into a place where he could do it. Or she could herself be a victim; perhaps the killer got rid of her body to preserve the impression that Craddock died accidentally and alone.

Or it all could be true; Bauer may have conspired with the killer, and then he may have turned on her after Craddock was dead. This is the most likely scenario in my eyes, primarily because of the fact that Benjamin called her.

I ask Laurie to call Tina Bauer's mother to see if we can come talk to her. I don't do it myself because Laurie's better than I am with distraught people; she's also better than I am with partially distraught or not at all distraught people.

In any event, the woman needs no convincing; she invites us to come right over. Laurie says that she seems thrilled that someone might finally listen to her.

Melinda Bauer lives in an apartment complex in Paterson called Kent Village. It will never be confused with a luxury condo, but the grounds are well kept and the apartments comfortable enough. Bauer buzzes us up to her third-floor apartment and stands waiting for us at the open door when we arrive.

"Come in, come in," she says before we can even introduce ourselves. "Do you have news about Tina?"

Laurie and I have decided that she will do most of the talking, for the same reason that she made the phone call. "Mrs. Bauer, we are investigating another case, and Tina's name has come up in connection with it."

"What other case?"

"We're not at liberty to say right now, but I can assure you that if our investigation turns up any information as to Tina's whereabouts, we will share that with you." There is no reason to tell her that the other case is a murder case; it will only upset her, and it is not proof that anything bad has happened to her daughter.

"Is she okay?"

"We're in the preliminary stages, but at this point, we have no knowledge of any harm that has come to her. You've reported to the police that she's missing?"

"Yes, I haven't heard a word from her in so long . . ."

"What did the police tell you?"

"That she is an adult and that they think she left on her own." She pauses and then says, more softly, "She's done it before."

"Run away?" Laurie asks.

A nod. "Yes."

"Had you gone to the police in the past when she ran away?"

"Yes." Then defensively, "I am her mother. I worry about her."

"We understand," Laurie says.

"Tina has had a difficult life. She got in with a bad crowd, and then there were drugs. And she and I . . . well, we've had our difficulties. I've tried my best, done all I can." She brightens. "But that is all behind her and us. I never saw her attitude so good."

"Do you know why that was?"

"She met a man. According to her, he was rich and important, and it was going to solve all our problems."

"Did she say the man's name?"

"She called him John. She never told me his last name. Do you think she ran off with him?"

Laurie tells her that we don't know what happened, and while that is technically true, I've got a feeling that Tina is never coming home.

"Did she ever mention the name Eric Benjamin?"

Mrs. Bauer shakes her head. "I don't believe so."

I have no doubt that the police attitude toward Tina's disappearance had to do with the fact that she had run away previous times and come home. Also, since Tina's mother knew her boyfriend's name only as John, the police had no reason to tie her to Craddock's death.

It took Kramer's investigating to start to do that.

Which in turn put Kramer in the crosshairs of the killers.

Kenny Zimmer's actions are troubling to me. I'm not talking about the fact that he lured my client onto the truck and attempted to kill him, though that is somewhat less than ideal behavior. The real question is, what the hell was he doing on the truck in the first place?

I buy that he answered George Davenport's Craigslist ad for the job; it was probably easy money, and my guess is that Zimmer rarely had two quarters to rub together. But then he got the $75,000 infusion and, according to his bar buddies, talked about that just being the beginning. For a guy like Zimmer, that would sound like an ideal time to quit his day job.

I doubt Zimmer was doing it for the dogs, so why continue? If he wanted to kill Dave Kramer, he could have come up with other venues to make the attempt. Maybe this was to be his last trip, but if that were the case, he gave no such indication to his boss, Davenport.

The dogs themselves continue to present another question: Where was he taking them? Sondra called every rescue group and shelter she could find in the northeast, and none of them knew anything about it. And since the rescue groups were the only source of money that Zimmer would be getting for delivering them, why was he bothering?

He had to be taking them somewhere; Zimmer doesn't sound like the type to be opening his own canine sanctuary. Maybe we just haven't successfully identified where they were to go, but the story has been in the media. If rescue groups were waiting for the dogs, why haven't they contacted us?

Sam calls, and his first sentence is a rather unappealing one. "I don't have great news."

"Let's hear it."

"Benjamin made only one call for the rest of the day after your lunch; it was to the Cayman Islands."

"Do you know who he called?"

"I have no idea and no way of finding out. He called a pay phone."

"Pay phone? They still have pay phones?"

"I guess so. I can tell you where the phone is, I can tell you that the call lasted for four minutes, but I can't tell you who answered the phone on the other end."

"Damn. Nothing else we can do?"

"No, but there are a couple of other things we know, for what it's worth. It's the seventh time Benjamin has called that number this month, and every call except one has been at 5:00 P.M. Eastern."

"Sam, email me the address of the pay phone, please."

"Will do."

I've already decided what I need to do. It's a sign of desperation, but that is appropriate in this situation because we're desperate. I'm going to send a member of our team to the Cayman Islands.

I realistically have four choices: Laurie, Marcus, Sam, or Hike. I can eliminate Laurie first. I need her here, and more importantly, I don't sleep with Marcus, Sam, or Hike.

I don't want to send Marcus for two reasons. First, it's not a job that requires a particular skill or expertise. Second, with Benjamin having threatened me, keeping Marcus close by seems like the smart move.

Sam could handle it easily enough, but his computer skills are absolutely and frequently crucial. Plus, the Bubalah Brigade needs his leadership.

Which leaves Hike. There's no question that he can handle it and that I can deal with the trial while he's gone. The only downside to Hike doing it is I have to speak to him about it. Hike doesn't usually react well in these situations; he even dreaded going to South Carolina when I sent him there. That is before he was voted South Carolinian of the Year.

But a man's got to do what a man's got to do, so I call him.

"Hike, I've got an assignment for you. It involves traveling."

"Good," he says, just about causing me to drop my phone. "I need to get away."

"Why?"

"Darlene and I split up, at least for now. It's to give her time to think. And now everywhere I look or go around here reminds me of her."

"How long was she here?"

"Almost two days."

"Well, then, a trip will do you good."

"Will I have to fly?"

"Yes."

"Will I have to switch planes?" Hike asks without even knowing where he will be going.

"Why? Is that a problem?" I'm already wishing I had chosen someone else to go.

"Twice as much chance of crashing. Either way, I want to be in coach . . . in the back."

"Why?" I ask.

"Planes don't back into mountains."

"Hike, are you at all interested in where you're going?"

"Of course."

"The Caymans."

"The Caymans? You mean the islands?"

"No, I mean Hank and Shirley Cayman's house in Vermont. Of course I meant the Cayman Islands, Hike. Fun in the sun."

"I don't know, Andy. Darlene has an aunt that lives on Long Island. We were going to invite her to the wedding."

"It's a different island, Hike. I don't think you'll run into her."

"Still . . . it might remind me of her," he says, clearly not convinced.

"Besides, Hike, you'll be too busy working to think about Darlene's Long Island aunt. Your mind will be occupied with other things."

"What do I have to do?"

"Watch a phone booth."

It's been four days since Hike left for the Caymans.

So far, the only positive development is that neither of his planes crashed. No one has received a 5:00 P.M. phone call on the pay phone, and Sam has verified that in his monitoring of Benjamin's calls.

I don't have Hike watching the phone all day, so there is always the possibility that someone else called the phone at a different time. But to have him watching constantly might be a red flag that the target might notice and then change his methods.

I'm finding that I'm missing Hike more than I'd expected in jury selection. He has good instincts, though it took me a while to develop a technique to understand them.

Hike basically thinks that every prospective juror will vote against us, so I used to just disregard his views. Then I realized they could be valuable as long as I utilized them based on gradations of his pessimism.

His opinions of each possible juror ranged from "absolute disaster" to "not a good choice for us." So when he said the former, then I would be more likely to shy away from that person. If his view was the latter, less strident one, then I'd see that person as someone to consider.

But I've muddled through, and we've picked twelve unlucky citizens and six almost as unlucky alternates. Seven women, nine whites, fairly elderly in composition . . . I think we've got a very good jury or a very bad one, depending on the verdict they ultimately reach.

Not only do these poor people have to put their lives on hold for however long the trial takes, but they are faced with one of three unpleasant outcomes. They can find Kramer guilty and then be afraid that they put an innocent man away for the rest of his life. Or they can find him not guilty and then be afraid they put a murderer back on the street. Or they can be hung and not come to a verdict, in which case they've simply wasted their and everybody else's time.

Kramer has been mostly silent and disengaged through the process. He's no dummy; I'm sure he views this as another step in what has felt like the system dragging him toward the edge of a cliff. The twelve people we have chosen are likely to be the ones who finally push him off.

We finish impaneling the jury at 3:00 P.M., and Judge Avery correctly thinks we should adjourn now and get started in the morning. I head home to have dinner with Laurie and Ricky. I'm not sure how often I'll get to do that during the trial.

Laurie has made my favorite, pasta amatriciana, and Ricky loves it as well. Tara and Sebastian aren't crazy about it, because it's not a food that we can slip them samples of.

After dinner Ricky joins me on the walk with Tara and Sebastian through Eastside Park. It's a cool early evening with a nice breeze. For the moment, all seems right with the world, and while that feeling is certain to be short-lived for me, I'm really enjoying it for right now.

Our walk takes more than an hour, longer than usual, because none of us want it to end. When we get home, Laurie is waiting for us on the porch. "Hike called," she says. "The call came in."

"What about Sam? Did you reach him?"

She nods. "I did. He confirmed that Benjamin made the call."

As soon as I get in the house, I call Hike. "Tell me all about it," I say.

"At five to five, this guy pulls up, driving a Mercedes. He gets out and walks to the phone, and five minutes later, it rings. I couldn't get close enough to hear what he was saying, but they talked for maybe six or seven minutes. Then he hung up, got in the car, and left."

"Great."

"I was going to follow him, but I did what you told me instead."

"You get the print?" I had arranged for Hike to have a fingerprint kit to take prints off the phone.

"I did. And then I wiped off the phone so there would be no sign that I did it. I scanned it and sent it to you; check your emails."

"Perfect."

"And I got the license plate; that's in the email as well. I'm pretty sure it's a rental car."

"Great job, Hike. Come back tomorrow. I need you in court."

"I will."

"Have a safe flight," I say.

"Flights," is how he corrects me. "There are two of them."

"I remember. And you're sure you don't want to upgrade to first class?"

"You know my feelings on that."

"Right . . . mountains. See you tomorrow, Hike."

I immediately check my email and call Pete. "Pete, I have a favor to ask."

"What else is new."

"There's a fingerprint that I need you to run."

"Forget it."

"I was hoping that as my favorite client, you'd have a more positive reaction." When Pete was himself wrongly accused of murder, I defended him, got him off, and didn't charge him a dime. I am not above reminding him of this fact occasionally when I need something.

"You're calling in a chip on a fingerprint?"

"Chips, Pete. I have many, many chips to use. We both know it."

He gives an exaggerated sigh, a sure sign that I've won. "Where's the print?"

"I'll email it to you."

Click. He hangs up on me, which in this case is a good sign.

That out of the way, I call Sam and give him the license plate number of the car used by the phone guy in the Caymans. "Can you find out who rented it?"

"If the rental car companies down there use computers. Any place that still has pay phones, you never know."

"Okay. Get me the name, and if I'm in court and you can't reach me, don't let that slow you down. Find out everything you can about the renter."

Roboton's offices are located on Route 9W in Englewood.

It's a sprawling, single-story building, very modern in design. Probably 70 percent of the exterior is glass. It's lucky the glass is tinted, or everyone in the place would be charcoal-broiled on a day like today. I'm here to see Steven Henderson, who has the title of acting CEO since the death of the founder of the company, John Craddock.

The receptionist brings me back to Henderson's office. I'd be surprised if he is thirty years old; my guess is that robotics is not a field with a lot of old people in it. He's dressed in jeans and a Penn State sweatshirt, so it's probably not a formal or fashion-conscious field, either.

"Welcome to the morgue," is his rather unusual opening line.

"Not sure I understand," I say.

"Let's just say that losing John was not exactly good for business. Which makes sense, since John was the business."

I tell him that I am representing Dave Kramer, which is what I had told him over the phone.

"He was here to see me," Henderson says. "He was asking about John."

"As am I." I decide to be straight with him. "I am operating under the assumption that John's death was not an accident."

Henderson nods. "That's what I figured when Kramer was here. But I'm afraid I'll be as little help to you as I was to him. Not only was

John a genius, but he was a well-liked genius. It seems very hard to believe he could have been murdered."

"You know Tina Bauer?"

He seems surprised by the question. Then, "I don't really know her, but I met her once. I'm afraid John was becoming more open about his women."

"That bothered you?" I ask.

He nods. "In a way. Have you met his wife, Christine? There's a lady who has been through enough and didn't deserve the humiliation."

"Have you had any contact with Tina Bauer since John died?"

He shakes his head. "None. But I don't know why I would." Then, "This was not the love of John's life that we're talking about. She was one in a series."

"Are you going to be the permanent CEO?" I ask.

He smiles. "If you're thinking I got rid of John to take his position, you might want to think again. Robotics is a business that depends on innovation and ideas and genius, and John provided all three. Everybody knows that; employees are already starting to leave. Unless we find someone to take his place, this company is history. And there is no one who can take his place."

"Did Craddock own a good portion of the stock?"

He nods. "Yes. The employees all had a small interest in it; John was good that way. But Christine, his wife, now owns 90 percent, which by next year at this time might as well be Confederate money, for all it will be worth."

"Are you exaggerating?"

He nods. "I guess so; I'm afraid I'm a little bitter. There are some patents that the company holds that are worth real money. But as an ongoing venture . . . I'm afraid not."

"And you said you're losing employees?"

"Some, but they're in a difficult place. If they leave, they lose their ownership interest, which is worth money if we sell the company."

"Are you planning to sell?" I ask.

"I'm afraid I can't discuss that," he says and then grins. "Unless you're here to make an offer."

"I forgot my checkbook. You said the employees are in a difficult place. Do they have other options?"

"Sure. If we go down, some other companies will fill the void. There are start-ups chomping at the bit right now. Robotics as an industry is not going away; it's exploding."

"What are you going to do?"

He smiles again. "I'm the captain; I'm going down with the ship. Besides, I owe everything I have to John. To leave now would feel like I'm abandoning his life's work."

Rodgers didn't get where he was . . . or even survive . . . because he was careless. On the contrary, there was no one who was more careful, who planned for every eventuality with more diligence, than Rodgers. It had served him well in the past, and it would serve him well now.

The other trait that had always been his trademark was a complete lack of trust. He had people working for him that were the absolute best at what they did. But they were used to being number one, to answer to no one but themselves, and they may well chafe at Rodgers's micromanaging style.

His people were smart, and they were tough, and they were not hindered by conscience or morals. Which meant that they were all candidates to turn on him. So he always had people watching them, and often he had people watching the watchers. It was an expensive way to do business, but ultimately worth it.

This was Rodgers's philosophy, the way he conducted his business and his life, and it was about to pay off again.

The call came from his person in the Caymans. His only function was to spy on Elway; he followed him wherever he went, had bugged his apartment, and had a tap on his phone. He was a thorough professional, and even someone as savvy as Elway had no idea any of it was happening.

"There have been some developments," he said. "Significant ones."

"Yes?" Rodgers asked.

"I told you that Elway has been taking the calls on the pay phone."

"Yes." Rodgers knew about the procedure and actually approved of the caution that Elway was displaying in doing so.

"After a call today, I was about to follow him, when I noticed someone else approach the phone. That person took fingerprints off the phone. There is no question that he was after Elway's prints."

"Were you able to identify the person?"

"Yes, through the car rental company. His name is Edward Lynch; he is a lawyer from New Jersey."

Rodgers knew exactly what that meant, and he knew that Elway's cover was blown, completely and permanently. Fortunately, though Elway still had some value, he had already accomplished most of his work. But that no longer mattered.

Elway had become a liability.

here is one thing that everyone in this courtroom can agree on. Judge Avery, Mr. Carpenter, the court reporter, the bailiff, and certainly myself . . . I don't think I'm going out on a limb when I say that we all understand that you have a crucial and tremendously important job to do. It is the cornerstone of our democracy, as important to who we are as voting."

Carla Westrum, I'm sorry to say, has an excellent court presence. She's speaks in a firm, confident voice and clearly has the ability to hold the attention of everyone in the room. She is likable, one of the reasons I don't like her.

She continues, "But important is not the same as difficult. Crucial is not the same as complicated. And the reason that I bring that up is because this case is not difficult, and it is certainly not complicated.

"Here are the facts that you will hear. The defendant, David Kramer, was convicted two years ago of assault against the victim, Kenneth Zimmer. Mr. Zimmer was hospitalized for his injuries. Mr. Kramer, perhaps in the bizarrely mistaken belief that he was the wronged party, then threatened Mr. Zimmer's life.

"Then, two years later, he followed through on that threat. Mr. Zimmer was working as a truck driver, transporting endangered dogs to where they could be rescued. Mr. Kramer boarded that truck and shot Mr. Zimmer to death. Mr. Zimmer was not armed.

"Then Mr. Kramer ran, and was ultimately captured by the police. That is it; that's the extent of it."

She pauses and shakes her head as if saddened by the horror of it all. "There is nothing that I have said, not one word, that I am not prepared to prove.

"But that is where you come in. You have to decide whether I have done what I've promised. If I have, then voting guilty will be obvious and necessary, and I am sure you will do your duty.

"And if I have not, then you will and should vote not guilty. That is how our system works, and it is the best system in the world. And you, for whatever time you are in this courtroom, are a vital part of it.

"Thank you."

We had gotten a late start this morning because the court heard various pretrial motions from both sides. Judge Avery was not inclined to grant any of the motions, which is the result I'd expected. We took a shot and tried to get him to keep out evidence of the previous assault on Zimmer by Kramer, but he wasn't buying it.

But it did bring the conclusion of Carla's opening statement to nearly lunchtime, which means Avery tells me that I should delay giving mine until the afternoon. That's fine with me; I don't want jurors hoping I'd hurry up and finish because they're hungry and they want to eat.

There's a message on my cell phone to call Sam, which I do. "Ready for this? The guy who answered the phone is using the name John Elway."

"That's not his real name?'

"Come on, Andy. John Elway used to be a quarterback for—"

I interrupt. "Trust me, Sam, I know who John Elway is. But it is possible that someone else has that name. He didn't copyright it."

"In this case it's fake. He's using a fake ID."

I don't bother asking Sam how he knows that; I don't need or want to know which laws he broke getting into which computers. I have this fear that someday I'll be defending Hilda Mandlebaum for illegal hacking. If she gets twenty years, that will take her to 106. I wonder if Eli will wait for her.

I thank Sam and ask him to see if he can learn anything else about Elway's actions in the Caymans, specifically in the area of banking. That's where the wired money to Zimmer came from, and it's very likely that Elway sent it.

Craddock's death was about money; I'd bet that Benjamin and the guy who calls himself Elway and who knows else saw profit in it. They were willing to put up $75,000 to Zimmer, but I have no doubt that's just the tip of the iceberg.

I can certainly assume that Craddock was personally worth a great deal of money. It would all go to his wife, so even though it's counter to my instinct, there is always the chance that she is involved.

If Steven Henderson is correct, then the company's value basically died with Craddock, so that couldn't be the motive. Of course, Henderson could be lying. He moved up to head of the company, so that always creates a suspicion.

But again, my instincts say otherwise.

I trust my instincts; I always have.

The trouble is that sometimes they are full of shit.

The final shipment arrived on time.

It was considerably smaller than previous shipments, because most of the weapons had arrived earlier. So the means of delivery was changed as well; it involved a risk, but a risk Rodgers was willing to take.

The building outside of Chesterfield, New Jersey, was soon to be what would likely be the most high-tech barn in the history of barns. Built to hold hay and horses and farm equipment, it was by now holding the means to change the world.

Rodgers had a lot of work ahead of him, but it was work that he was competent to handle, and it was easy to undertake.

Remember the first day you came to this court-room?" is how I begin my opening statement. "This room, and the anteroom next door, were packed with people. I checked, and a hundred and fourteen people were considered to fill the seats that you're in. And from out of that large group, the twelve of you were selected. Have you wondered why?

"Well, I'm going to tell you. You were chosen for two main reasons. Number one, Ms. Westrum and I had confidence that you could be unbiased. We felt you could come in here without any predispositions and judge the facts and render a fair verdict to the best of your ability.

"Now don't misunderstand me; I would have been fine if you had been biased for the defense. And I don't want to speak for Ms. Westrum, but I suspect that she might have been okay with you being biased for the prosecution. But neither of us would have allowed you to be part of the jury if we thought you favored the other side.

"Now the other reason you are here, and it is crucial, is that we thought you could use your logical minds to analyze the evidence. And that logic is what I am counting on.

"The prosecution is going to tell you exactly what happened; Ms. Westrum has already told you that the facts are so clear that your verdict should be obvious. But you know what? None of it makes sense.

"In her version, people do exactly what they shouldn't do, and they act exactly against their own interests. What you would be asked to believe fails the logic test. And the reason it fails is because it didn't happen that way.

"David Kramer has spent much of his life in law enforcement. Before that, he was a fighter pilot in the United States Air Force. He has risked his life countless times to protect you, and me, and Ms. Westrum, and everyone else in this courtroom.

"He is also smart and obviously wise in the ways of law enforcement. There is no possible way he could have acted in the way the prosecution would have you believe.

"But his service and his smarts would not matter if he committed this crime. If he did, you should and would still vote guilty, and you would be right to do so.

"But he did not."

When I get back to the defense table, Kramer leans over to me and says, "You're as good as advertised."

"Nothing said so far matters," I say. "Trial starts Monday."

As soon as I get out of court, I check my phone for messages, hoping that Sam has come up with more information on the guy called Elway.

There are four messages. The first is from Hike, telling me that he survived both flights and that he is home if I need him. The second is from Pete, telling me to meet him at Charlie's. The third is from Laurie, telling me to meet Pete at Charlie's. The fourth is from Pete, telling me that he's waiting for me at Charlie's.

I have a feeling I'm supposed to meet Pete at Charlie's.

There are two possibilities that I can think of for why Pete called this meeting. It could be that he has significant information for me, hopefully the results of the fingerprints Hike sent from the Caymans. Elway can fake an ID, but he can't fake a print.

Or it's possible that Charlie's won't let Pete charge burgers and beer to my tab anymore, and Pete doesn't want me—he wants my wallet.

But the fact that Laurie is on board with me meeting him there makes me discount this as a possibility.

It's only five thirty when I get to Charlie's, but the place is fairly crowded. At seven, when the Mets and Yankees games start, it will be packed. Friday is always a busy night.

Pete is at our regular table, but Vince is not here yet. He usually shows up right around the time of the first pitch. To be here now would mean he'd be stuck for an hour and a half with nothing to complain about. He would have to talk, and human interaction is not something that Vince excels at.

"This better be good," I say. "I could be having dinner with Laurie and Ricky."

"I'm sure they'll survive the disappointment. Where did you get that print?"

"Whose is it?" I ask.

"Where did you get it?"

"Whose is it?" I ask again. Then, "We seem to be at an impasse."

"This is serious stuff, Andy."

"Maybe so, but I have the advantage. I have other ways of finding out whose fingerprint that is, but you have no other way of knowing where I got it. So whose is it?"

I know Pete really well, so I can tell when he's mad. He's mad now. He stares at me, and in the next ten seconds, he is either going to tell me or shoot me.

"His name is Bennett Jeffries. Does that name mean anything to you?"

"I know I've heard it, but I can't place the context."

"He's wanted for bank fraud, money laundering, illegal arms sales, and aiding and abetting terrorists. And I just told you the highlights. I ran the print through the national database, and it lit up like a damn Christmas tree. The feds called me before I even got the report. They want to meet with you."

"When?"

"Tomorrow morning, 9:00 at the Newark FBI office."

"Ricky has a baseball game tomorrow morning. Move the meeting to eleven."

"That's not funny."

"I don't mean it to be. Look, I've got a client to defend; right now, that is all I care about. So if I have information that the government needs, I will use that to leverage something for my client. I have the upper hand here. But I haven't figured out what I want yet, so for now,

I'll just use my immense power to move the meeting to eleven so I can see my son's baseball game."

"You realize you are now screwing around with the federal government? They don't care if you buy them beer and hamburgers."

"Wow . . . the federal government? That is really scary. I hope they don't yell at me at our eleven o'clock meeting."

"You truly are a pain in the ass."

I nod. "That's been pointed out to me so many times that I've come to terms with it."

"Now where did you get the print?" Pete asks.

"If I tell you now, do I have your absolute word that you will not tell anyone else?"

"Of course not," he says.

"Then you'll find out when they do. If they do."

'**ve** come to terms with the fact that Ricky will never play in the majors.

I think I first realized that last year when he struck out in T-ball. If you can't hit a ball placed waist high, sitting stationary on a tee, it's unlikely you're going to develop to the point where you can hit a ninety-eight-mile-an-hour fastball, or a ninety-one-mile-an-hour slider.

But the final proof is that Ricky has failed the right field test. I would bet that in our entire history there has never been a major-league ballplayer who as a youth was consigned to right field in Little League. It is where they hide mediocrity, the place where they put kids and then pray that no one hits the ball to them.

Right field is, quite simply, oblivion. It is the Siberia of baseball positions. The NFL equivalent would be playing for the Cleveland Browns.

And yes, Ricky is in right field. He doesn't seem to understand the ignominy of it all, which I am glad about. Nor does he seem to resent that his best friend, Will Rubenstein, is the shortstop, fielding ground balls and hitting line drives like Derek Jeter.

For a while I blamed the coach and searched for a solution. I had options; for example, I could have moved our family to another city and, therefore, a different Little League team. Or I could have asked Marcus to kill the coach, or at least see to it that he was hospitalized and had to be replaced.

But Laurie made me see the light, probably by telling me that I was an idiot and a lunatic. It also helped that Ricky was so obviously having fun. So if he can't be a major leaguer, maybe he can do something lesser but also important, like doctor or college professor.

After the game, I tell Ricky how well he did, and I specifically do not mention that he has killed my life's dream. We drove here with Tara and Sebastian, but since this Eastside Park field is quite close to our house, Laurie and Ricky will walk them home while I take the car to my eleven o'clock meeting in Newark.

Pete offered to pick me up, but I declined. If he doesn't like the way the meeting goes, he wouldn't be above leaving me at a bus stop.

The meeting is at the FBI's Newark office, and Pete is waiting for me in the lobby when I get there. It's five to eleven, but the first thing he says is, "Where the hell have you been?" Not a good start.

"Come on," he adds, and I follow him back to the conference room where we are meeting. He knows his way around. I've been here before but don't have the slightest idea where I'm going.

Waiting for us in the room is a group of seven FBI agents, all wearing the same suit. The lead guy for their contingent is Jeffrey Givens, whom I've dealt with on a case before. It ultimately worked out well for everyone involved, but getting there was like having a root canal. The positive is that we both know each other's negotiating style.

Givens introduces me to his colleagues, but since I will never be able to remember their names, I don't even bother trying. They either all have a function here, in which case the FBI considers this matter very important, or they want to impress me with their seriousness, in which case the FBI considers this matter very important.

That leaves me with one inescapable conclusion: the FBI considers this matter very important. Once we're all seated, Givens says, "Well, here we are again."

I look around and say, "Some of my fondest memories were created in this very room."

Givens turns to the agent next to him and says, "I told you so." Then, to me, "You asked Captain Stanton to run a fingerprint."

He stops, as if expecting an answer, but since it wasn't a question, I just wait for him to continue.

He does. "The print is from a man who is currently a wanted criminal, with numerous warrants out for his arrest. We have a need to know where you retrieved the print."

"Who is he?" I ask. I had told Pete that I would not hang him out to dry by revealing that he'd told me the print belonged to Bennett Jeffries. It's also a test to see how up-front Givens will be with me.

"His name is Bennett Jeffries."

My instinct in these situations is to be difficult, mainly because I get more that way. But the problem here is that I don't know what I want to get, beyond general help in the defense of my client. I don't even know if these guys are in a position to provide such help.

The other difficulty I face, which weakens my position even if the FBI doesn't realize it, is that I have no productive way to proceed with Jeffries. I know he's down in the Caymans, and I know he's in some kind of conspiracy with Benjamin, but I don't know how to get beyond that.

"Is this conversation being recorded?" I ask.

He nods. "It is."

"I'm sure you'll understand that my obligation is to my client."

"Not to your country," he says, a hint of righteous scorn in his voice.

"To the legal system of my country, which tells me that my obligation is to my client."

"What do you have to gain by not giving us this information?" he asks.

"Actually, that's not quite the way I would phrase the question. I would ask what do I have to gain by giving it to you? And you can leave out the part about service to my country."

"You're aware that if I directly ask you for this information, and you lie or refuse to provide it, you are committing a crime?"

"Unless I were to say that it was mailed to me anonymously or the fingerprint fairy gave it to me. Or I might walk out of this office and tell you that I am not talking to you voluntarily, and you can send me a grand jury subpoena. And then I'd whisper under my breath that you can shove the fingerprint directly up your ass."

I'm definitely on shaky ground here in that he's right; it is illegal to lie to law enforcement or to withhold information that they directly ask for. He hasn't actually asked me yet, which may be by design. We are both keeping all of our options.

"What are you looking for?" he asks.

"Putting his whereabouts to the side for the moment, this guy Jeffries is involved in a conspiracy that has resulted in my client being wrongly accused of a murder." I steal a quick glance at Pete to see if he's reacting to my comment, since he is the "wrong accuser," but he's stone-faced.

I continue, "At least one of the coconspirators is Eric Benjamin. Benjamin's fingerprint was found on the truck where the murder was committed." Neither Givens nor anyone else reacts to this; I'm assuming they know who Benjamin is, but I can't be sure.

"If it turns out that I know where Jeffries is, and I tell you, then you are going to arrest him. You are also going to take his life apart and examine every move he has made. You will uncover things that can help my client. I need your word that you will share whatever you learn with me."

Givens makes eye contact with someone, who nods ever so slightly. Maybe Givens is not the top guy in the room after all. "Okay."

"I have just one more question before I become the answer man."

"You're a pain in the ass," Givens says, making it unanimous, and for the first time, I see Pete nod in agreement.

"Stipulated. So here's the question: You could have called me in to your office, sat me across from your desk, and asked me where Jeffries is. Instead, you assembled an entire platoon of FBI agents here to observe the process. Which leads me to believe there is an urgency to this. What might that be?"

Givens hesitates and says, "There is an urgency. We have reason to believe Jeffries is involved in something that can be very dangerous to a lot of people."

"And what might that be?" I ask again.

"That's all I'm going to tell you. Now I'll ask you directly, where was Jeffries when you got his fingerprint?"

I've extracted all I'm going to get; it's time to hold up my end of the bargain.

"The Cayman Islands. I can give you the name he's using and where he's living."

"Please do," he says.

C all your first witness," Judge Avery says.

Carla stands, a serious, somber expression on her face, and says, "The state calls Mr. John Paxos." Churchill spoke with less drama in his "blood, sweat, and tears" speech.

Paxos, a pleasant-looking man who is probably nearing retirement age, walks up to the stand and agrees to tell the truth and nothing but the truth.

Game on.

Paxos is there to set the scene. He discovered Zimmer's body on the truck, but his testimony is not crucial. He has no special knowledge essential to solving the crime; he just happened to be the first one there after it happened.

"Mr. Paxos, where were you on August 14, at around 1:00 P.M.?"

"I stopped in a rest area off the Garden State Parkway, near Exit 156."

"Why did you stop there?"

He smiles with some embarrassment. "To use the bathroom. I had been driving a long time."

"Were there any other vehicles parked there when you arrived?"

"Yes. A large tractor trailer; but I didn't see the driver."

Carla painstakingly takes Paxos through his trip to the bathroom, then his curiosity about the truck, hearing the barking, finally entering it and seeing Zimmer's body, and calling animal control and then 911.

She chronicles his every move with the exception of zipping up his fly in the bathroom; if she continues at this pace through the trial, we're going to be here a very long time. I think I see one of the jurors grimace, but it could be a gas pain.

Finally, she reluctantly turns the witness over to me. There's really nothing for me to gain from his testimony, since it neither hurt nor helped us. "Mr. Paxos, that must have been an upsetting experience for you."

"You mean testifying just now?" he asks.

I smile. "That too," I say, and the jurors and those seated in the gallery laugh. "But I'm talking about that day at the rest stop."

"Sorry. Yes, it was."

"Did you see anyone besides the victim at the rest stop? I mean, before you made your phone calls for assistance."

"No."

"For all you know, there could have been twenty people there before you arrived?"

"Yes," he says.

"A marching band could have come through there?"

"Yes."

Carla objects, but since Paxos has already answered, the point is moot. Judge Avery cautions him to pause before he answers, in case the lawyers want to object.

"You said that you thought the truck was parked in an unusual position, did you not?"

He waits a while because of Judge Avery's instructions; the effect is as if he's testifying via satellite, with a delay. "I did."

"Can you describe that for us, please?"

Another exaggerated delay, and then, "Well, the parking spaces outside the building are perpendicular to it, you know what I mean? If you park there, you're facing the building directly. But the truck was at an angle, so it was taking up like . . . I don't . . . at least seven of the spaces. And it wasn't against the curb, it was backed away from it. I had to park around the corner from it because it didn't leave me any room."

"You said that when the dogs heard you, they started to bark."

"Right."

"How long did it take them to stop barking?"

"I don't think they did, at least not all of them. Then people started showing up, so they started again."

"But they apparently had had enough time to calm down from whatever happened before you made the noise?" I want to convey the idea that Paxos got there well after the killing, because I want there to have been enough time for the third person, Eric Benjamin, to have gotten away.

"Yes, I guess so," he says.

"Thank you. No further questions."

Carla calls Ralph Brandenberger to the stand to testify to his actions and observations that day. Ralph has nothing to add of an evidentiary nature; he didn't discover the body, nor did he have any role related to the scene once he got there. All he did was show up to possibly care for the dogs.

But Carla is no dummy. She questions Ralph about the dogs in great detail. She clearly wants the jury to see Zimmer as a savior of stray, helpless animals. The more sympathetic the victim, the more the jury will want to identify and punish his killer.

I ask Ralph very little on cross-examination, just enough to reassure the jurors that the dogs are fine and that nothing bad happened to them. Carla objects when Ralph refers to me and the Tara Foundation as the dogs' rescuers, but Avery overrules her. The facts are the facts.

The morning session is over, and in basketball terms, we have suffered "no harm, no foul."

That's going to change.

I head to the cafeteria for a quick lunch but stop to check my phone messages. The first one is Givens, from the FBI, telling me it was important that he hear from me ASAP.

I call him and am immediately put through.

"I need to see you right away."

"I'm in court."

"Can you get out of it?"

"Sure. Give me a note. Just write, 'Andy can't come to court today because he has a cold.'"

"You really are a pain in the ass," he says.

"And you need to get new material. What's going on?"

"When can you be here?"

"Five o'clock. Is it going to be just you or the dark-suited gang of seven?"

"Just me. Five o'clock."

have no idea what Givens wants and no time to worry about it.

Carla is about to call a bunch of witnesses who will make it obvious to the jury that Kramer committed murder.

The fact is that whatever Givens wants, he's going to be disappointed. I'm quite sure he's not calling me in to give me information I can use; he wouldn't have been so anxious to meet right away. But I've got nothing else to give him, much like I have nothing else to give the jury. When it comes to Givens, my negotiating gun is unloaded.

Carla's next witness is Alan Delaney of the state highway department. All he is here for is to say that he retrieved the rest stop video from the time in question and gave it to Captain Pete Stanton. He's a chain-of-custody witness and so unimportant that I don't even question him.

Next is Sergeant Tom Quaranto, who executed a search warrant on Kramer's house. He testifies that he originally went to the house to take Kramer into custody, but he wasn't home. He waited there for forty-five minutes until a search warrant could be secured, at which point he went in. Kramer's handgun was on the kitchen table, and Quaranto confiscated it. He says that it was obvious that it had recently been fired.

On cross, I ask, "Sergeant Quaranto, how did you know that Mr. Kramer was not at home?"

"There was a note on the door to that effect. I also rang the bell and knocked on the door. I still wasn't positive he wasn't home; he could have been deliberately avoiding us. But it turned out that he wasn't there."

I introduce the note that Kramer had left as evidence and ask him to read it. It clearly says that he is at the home of his attorney, Andy Carpenter, and it gives my address. At the time he wrote it, I wasn't his attorney, but I don't think I'll point that out to the jury.

"So he told you where to find him?" I ask.

"Yes."

"And was he telling the truth? Was he in fact at my house?"

He nods. "I believe he was, yes."

"Do you often get that kind of information from fugitives?"

"Every case is different," he says, avoiding my question.

"Thanks for sharing that," I say. "Have you ever had a fugitive leave a note to tell you exactly where he is?"

I get a grudging "no" from Quaranto.

"Were you surprised that he wrote the note in the first place, since it shows he knew you were coming for him?"

"Somewhat."

"Were you surprised that he left his gun out where you could easily find it?"

"No. We would have found it by thoroughly searching the house wherever he hid it."

"If he had thrown it in the Passaic River, would you have found it by thoroughly searching the house?"

"No."

"So just to recap, he told you where to find him, and he placed his gun in a location where you couldn't miss it. Is that accurate?"

"Yes."

"Did you send him a thank-you note for making your job so much easier?"

Carla objects, and Judge Avery sustains . . . business as usual. It doesn't matter; my point was made.

"No further questions. Thank you."

Sergeant Rebecca Camp is next in line in the boring witness parade. She ran the ballistics tests on the gun and determined it was

Kramer's. She also ran tests on the bullet that killed Zimmer, which showed that it came from Kramer's gun.

It does not come as a shock that she testifies to all of this. She comes off as a competent, credible witness, and she also has the advantage of being correct.

My approach with witnesses like this is simple. I can't shake them or cast doubt on their credibility, because the facts are not in my favor. But I don't want to let them off completely unscathed, because I don't want a prosecution steamroller effect to be generated.

"Sergeant Camp, do you know who fired that weapon?"

"You mean when Mr. Zimmer was shot?"

"Yes," I say.

"I do not."

"Do you know the circumstances under which it was fired?"

"What do you mean?"

"Well, for example, was the shooter lying in wait to gun down his victim? Or was it self-defense? Did the shooter use his left hand or his right? Was the victim blindfolded and given a final cigarette? That's what I mean. Any circumstances at all. Do you know anything about the shooting other than that there was a shooting and this was the gun used?"

Carla objects that I'm badgering the witness, which I am. Judge Avery overrules the objection and lets her answer the question, but admonishes me.

"I have no knowledge as to any of that one way or the other," she says.

"Thank you."

It's 4:00 P.M., and since Judge Avery has now learned that in Carla's hands there is no such thing as a quick witness, he adjourns for the day. I call Laurie and tell her I'll be late, that I've been called to another meeting at the FBI.

"Do you know why?" she asks.

"No. It could be that they just like having me around, because of my bubbly personality."

"No," she says. "It couldn't."

Givens was telling the truth; he's alone waiting for me in his office.

"How's your trial going?" he asks.

"A laugh a minute."

"I assume your client is innocent?" he asks in a tone that says that he believes the opposite.

I nod. "Pure as the driven snow."

"Who actually got Elway's fingerprint off the phone in the Caymans?"

"I guess we're done shooting the breeze. It was an attorney in my firm, Hike Lynch."

"Could he have done anything to alert Jeffries to the fact that he was onto him?"

"Why? Did Jeffries disappear?"

"Could you please answer the question?" he asks.

"Obviously, he could have made a mistake, but he said he didn't, and he's a smart guy. He waited until Jeffries got in his car and left, and then a few minutes later, he went to the phone and got the print. Then he washed off the phone so that no one could tell what he had done."

"You're sure of all this?"

"I'm sure that's what he told me. And I'm sure that those were my instructions to him when he went down there. And I'm sure he would have no reason to lie to me."

Givens nods; I'm sure he expected me to tell him all of this. "Well, something spooked Elway, because he's nowhere to be found."

"It could be a coincidence."

"I don't think so."

I nod. "I don't either. But I really doubt that Hike did anything that would result in this."

There's a knock on the door, and another agent opens it and asks if he could speak to Givens outside for a moment. Givens tells me he'll be right back and goes out into the hall with the agent. This would be a good opportunity for me to look through the papers on his desk, except for the fact that there are no papers on his desk.

It's probably five minutes before he returns. "They found Jeffries."

"Glad to hear it."

"His body washed up on the shore."

"Oh."

"I'm going to level with you, and if I find out you revealed any of what I'm about to tell you, your body will be the next one to turn up on a beach," he says. "We had information that Jeffries had arranged the purchase of some dangerous weapons. They might be meant for domestic use. We don't know where, or when, or even why."

"Mushroom cloud–type weapons?" I ask.

"No, thank God."

"Why are you telling me this?"

"Because we were searching for Jeffries for months, and you found him before we could. So whatever your sources of information, or your methods, if they turn up more relevant information, I want it."

"Our deal is still in place," I say.

He nods. "Yes, it is."

"Then I have nothing right now," I say. "But if I get anything, it's yours."

I spend the drive home trying to make sense out of all this. It seems very likely that Hike's uncovering Jeffries's whereabouts and identity led to his death. It's not certain; there is always the possibility that his death was unrelated to Hike retrieving the print. But that would be way up on the coincidence scale, substantially past my belief level, and apparently past the FBI's as well.

My view is that Eric Benjamin, and his coconspirators, believed that Kramer was a threat to them. They tried to kill him, and when that failed, they framed him in order to take him out of commission.

Then Tina Bauer either helped them kill John Craddock or was a witness to it. Either way, she is gone, and I have my doubts that she is alive.

Now Bennett Jeffries, likely one of the key conspirators, was himself killed because his partners thought he was about to be exposed.

If Craddock was murdered, and I believe that he was, then there are only two possible reasons that I can think of. One is money, but the fact that his wife inherited most of it, and that his company has deteriorated in his absence, makes that hard to understand.

The other possibility is the nature of the company itself. Perhaps Craddock's genius in robotics was somehow threatening to the conspiracy.

The drive isn't long enough for me to figure out what's going on. I could drive to Tibet, and it wouldn't be long enough.

This is not going to be a fun weekend.

              I will spend it going over all the documents related to the case and preparing to cross-examine the prosecution witnesses that are coming up. Of course, now that the football season has begun, my preparation will pause on Sunday at one o'clock to watch the Giants game.

Saturday morning, I settle down in the den with the documents, but first I open yesterday's mail, which I had not gotten to. It's just a few bills and two letters from credit card companies congratulating me on being preapproved. I'm humbled by their confidence in me and touched that they are willing to do all of this for only 25.99 percent interest.

There's also a statement from my broker, Edna's cousin Freddie. It's a notice informing me that he sold our shares in Victor's Donuts, as per our direction. Laurie will be pleased to know we no longer own any part of "that complete and total pig's company."

I open it and see that all of our previous profits on the stock had disappeared, and then some. Victor Andreson's arrest and removal from the company caused investors to decide to bail out. By the time we joined them, we had taken a big hit.

The stock fiasco reminds me of the situation at Roboton after Craddock's death. I call Freddie at home and tell him I want to talk to him about the sale.

"You having second thoughts?" he asks. "Because we could buy it back for what we sold it."

"No, I wanted to ask you about something you said last time we talked. You said you wish we had been short the stock."

"Right."

"What does that mean?" I ask.

"You short a stock when you think it's going to go down. What you're doing is borrowing the shares, then you sell them, but you have an obligation to return them to the person you borrowed them from. If the stock goes down, you buy them back at the lower price so you can return them. The difference is your profit."

"Freddie, I don't have the slightest idea what you're talking about."

He sighs. "Okay, let's say stock A is twenty dollars a share. I own one hundred shares, and you borrow them from me. You then sell them for twenty dollars each. You expect the stock to go down, which is why you're doing it. So it does go down to ten dollars. You then buy it back at the ten-dollar price and return the stock to me."

"So I originally sold it for twenty, and bought it back for ten," I say.

"Right. The ten-dollar difference per share is your profit."

"Are you familiar with a company called Roboton?"

"Of course. That was John Craddock's company."

"Could someone have shorted that stock and in the process made a lot of money when he was killed?"

"No," he says.

"That's not the answer I was looking for. Just for future reference, when I ask a question like that, I'm hoping for *yes*."

"Sorry, Andy. You know I don't like to disappoint you, but the answer is a definite no. It's just not possible."

"Why not?"

"Because Roboton is a privately held company. The Craddock family owns almost all the shares. I believe the employees own the rest. You can't short a stock that isn't publicly traded."

"That's unfortunate," I say.

"Andy, what are you looking for? Maybe I can help."

"I've been trying to find someone who profited from Craddock's death and the effect of that death on his company."

"Well, then, I've got good news for you," he says. "You did."

"What do you mean?"

"You have some shares in a stock called Sky Robotics; I got a bunch of my clients a small piece of it in the IPO. You were one of them, but you don't have that much of it. I wish you had more."

"It went up when Craddock died?"

"Way up. They were working on similar products, very competitive. Two of Craddock's employees actually left to go to Sky when he died."

"So Sky is a public company?" I ask.

"Yes. IPO stands for *initial public offering*. That's what you do when you open up the company to public ownership."

"How much did it go up in value?"

"Market cap?" he asks.

"I don't know what that means."

"Market capitalization. It's the number of shares times the value of each share. It shows what the company is valued at."

"I just want to know how much Sky Robotics was worth before John Craddock died and after he died."

"Market cap. I'd have to check. Can you hold on a minute?"

"Sure."

He takes twice that time, but Freddie finally comes back. "Sorry, took longer than I thought. Here it is. The day John Craddock died, Sky Robotics had a market cap estimated at seven hundred million. Today, it is a billion nine."

"So Sky gained over a billion dollars because John Craddock died?"

"I can't say that it is all attributable to that, but I bet a lot of it is."

"Freddie, you're a genius."

He laughs. "Andy, you do realize that most of that billion is not yours, right?"

"Even if I made only a half billion, I'm happy," I say. Then I thank him, hang up, and go into the kitchen to tell Laurie what I've learned.

Laurie thinks it's definitely a viable possibility that Craddock's murder was designed to bring down his company so someone could profit from the downfall. But she adds a note of caution, pointing out, "We can't even be positive that Craddock was murdered."

"He was."

"Can you prove it in court?"

"No."

"There's one other thing, Andy. Even if we're close to proving Crad-dock was murdered and close to proving a motive, how does that help us convince the jury that Dave is innocent?"

"Laurie, if you're going to insist on using logic and reality, I'm not going to be able to talk to you anymore."

Robbie Divine is one of the richest men in the country.

I met him at a charity dinner once, and we've become sort of friends. I think he hangs out with me so he can understand how the peasant class lives.

Robbie knows more about markets and money than anyone I know, and I've called on his expertise a few times to help with cases. He once confided in me that he loves money, literally loves it, but is bothered by the fact that he can never have all of it.

I call him at home, although I have no idea what home he is in. Robbie has it set up that when someone dials his Manhattan apartment number, it rings in all of his homes. At last count he had seven of them, four in the US and one each in Anguilla, London, and Hong Kong.

"It's two thirty in the morning," he says, instead of *hello*. He sounds wide awake.

"Hong Kong?" I ask.

"Hong Kong. What the hell do you want?"

"Are you familiar with Sky Robotics?"

"Why do you insult me?" he says. "From now on, just assume that I am familiar with every company that has a market cap higher than your average convenience store."

"I know what market cap means."

"Congratulations. What about Sky Robotics?"

"Do you own a piece of it?"

"No," he says. "And I remain pissed about that."

"Why?"

"Because I was all set to participate in the IPO in a major way, and then Greg Hepner came up with outside money. Then the damn thing took off."

"Who is Greg Hepner?" I ask.

"I can see you've really studied this company in depth. He's the CEO and chairman of Sky Robotics."

"Where did the outside money come from?" I ask.

"It was foreign money. A private equity company I had never heard of."

"Was it legit?" I ask.

"I have my doubts."

"What is your relationship like with Hepner?"

"When I didn't get to participate in the IPO, I told him I wouldn't piss on him if he were on fire."

"So you can't get me in to see him?"

"Of course I can get you in. Next year, he may need my money."

"Can you get me in tomorrow? I know it's Sunday, but I'm back in court on Monday."

"Call me back at noon. My time," he says and then hangs up.

When I call Robbie back at 11:00 P.M., which is 11:00 A.M. in Hong Kong, he answers the phone with, "The son of a bitch won't meet with you."

"Why not?"

"He said he's traveling starting this morning."

"You sound like you don't believe him," I say.

"I don't. He was very friendly when I called, and as soon as I mentioned your name, he got all uptight. I think he's afraid of you."

"I'm a scary guy," I say.

"Don't I know it."

Today is video day. Unfortunately, it's a movie that I've seen already.

In fact, I've probably watched it fifteen times, but it never gets better.

It's the video from the rest stop on the day of the murder, and it will be introduced by the technician who set up the security system. It shows Dave Kramer pull up in his car. He goes into the restroom and then comes out. No one else has arrived, so Kramer stands at the curb for six excruciating minutes, waiting.

Finally, the tractor trailer pulls up on the other side, parking at that weird angle. Kramer waits for about fifteen seconds, then walks around the side of the building to the truck.

He stands at the door to the truck and then opens it. It looks as if his mouth is moving, but there is no audio on the tape, so it's impossible to be sure and obviously impossible to hear what he might be saying.

Finally, he looks around and then steps onto the truck. Fortunately, there is no sign of him drawing his weapon before he steps on. I would assume that there was a lot of barking going on at that point, but obviously the people in the court can't hear that. They also can't hear the gunshot that we all know must have rung out. Somehow the silence seems to make it worse, if that's possible.

Forty seconds after he stepped onto the truck, Kramer comes off. He does not look stressed or upset, and certainly one would never guess he had just warded off an attack on his life by shooting and killing his attacker. Not a great look for our side.

There is still no sign of the gun. He just seems to calmly look around to make sure there is no one else there. Then he quickly walks back around to his car and drives off.

The tape then continues for almost five minutes, focused on the truck but showing absolutely no movement of anything or anyone. Clearly, Carla has anticipated the possibility of our relying on the "third person" defense and is using the tape to refute it.

The jury seems mesmerized by it, never taking their eyes off the screen. There is no question that it is devastating; no one watching it would find anything inconsistent with the accusation that Dave Kramer is a cold-blooded murderer. It's not a smoking gun, but it's definitely a smoking tape.

A second tape is shown, this time of John Paxos arriving at the rest stop and ultimately getting onto the truck. It's unnecessary to the prosecution's case, in that it merely confirms what Paxos has said, and nobody would have doubted his version in the first place.

But it does seem to emphasize the coldness Kramer displayed in leaving the truck there, with dogs locked in cages and a dead or dying Zimmer on the floor.

When the entire show is over, Carla has no questions for the witness, implying correctly that the tapes speak for themselves. My cross-examination consists of one question. I ask if this was the only camera and therefore the only angle. The answer is yes.

I look over at Kramer, and I can tell that he's shaken by what he's just seen. It's not that it's inconsistent with the story we have to tell; it's that it is obvious how difficult it will be to get anyone to believe our version.

Next up on Carla's hit parade is Janet Carlson, the Passaic County coroner. She is here to testify to the cause and estimated time of death. Janet is a very competent coroner, and this case didn't exactly cause her to stretch her abilities very much.

She attributes the death to a single bullet fired into Zimmer's heart. As to the time, she can't be precise, but it generally matches up to the time Kramer was there, as shown on the tape.

Carla's main goal here, which she accomplishes quite well, is to introduce photographs of the crime scene inside the truck. The amount of blood lost by Zimmer is very substantial; a bullet in the heart will do that. So the scene is gory, and she wants the jury to see it in full color.

An added bonus for her is that some of the photographs show dogs still in their cages. Just in case there are any dog lovers on the jury, and the odds are that there certainly must be some, this seems to add a bit more horror to what they believe Kramer has done.

All in all, it's hard to picture a more depressing court day. Carla spent it perched on top of the legal hill, firing artillery down on us. We were cowering in our foxhole, unable to return fire, and just wishing for the barrage to end.

And tomorrow should be worse.

Greg Hepner's code name was Brady, and Brady was worried.

He was so worried that he placed a call to Rodgers, despite being told that was to be done only in an urgent situation. Brady believed that this was nothing if not urgent.

"This is Brady. I—"

"I know who it is," Rodgers said. He was instantly annoyed. Rodgers had a considerable amount of disdain for Brady and would have preferred to have used someone else. Brady was gutless and prone to panic, which made no sense, since his part of the operation was concluded a long time ago.

"I got a phone call; Kramer's lawyer, Carpenter, wants to talk to me."

"What did you say?"

"I said no; I made up an excuse that I was traveling."

"Why did you do that?" Rodgers asked.

"I don't know what he knows."

"He knows nothing."

"Then why the hell does he want to talk to me?" Brady asked, raising his voice more than he'd wanted to. He lowered it and tried to calm himself, saying, "He must know something. Otherwise what could I have to do with his case?"

"He's grasping at straws."

"Maybe, but right now, I'm the straw he's grasping at."

Rodgers considered telling Brady to contact Carpenter and arrange the meeting, but Brady was too prone to panic. He might say the wrong thing.

"I'll handle this," Rodgers said, and hung up.

Rodgers thought about the situation for more than an hour. It was his style; he prided himself on never taking precipitous action. But once he came to a decision, he never questioned it or hesitated.

He called Eric Benjamin, otherwise known as Manning. "Carpenter has become a problem," he said.

"I don't know what we can do about him. Getting rid of him would call too much attention to things; it would be front-page news. And it might even get Kramer off the hook."

"I don't care about Kramer," Rodgers said. "I don't know why you have never understood that he doesn't matter. Carpenter is the only one even close to being in position to put it all together before we make our move. And once we make that move, nothing matters."

"Are you saying that we should remove Carpenter?"

"No. I'm saying *you* should remove Carpenter."

Jessica Martinez expected to testify years ago . . . not now. She was Kenny Zimmer's girlfriend back then and was hiding in an adjoining room when Dave Kramer paid him a visit the first time around. She witnessed their confrontation and became the key witness against Kramer when subsequent charges were filed.

She never got to testify then, because Kramer copped a plea to a misdemeanor. I can imagine that was fine with her; I'm sure Kramer doesn't seem like a guy she would want as an enemy.

Yet here she is.

Carla calls Martinez to the stand. I know what she is going to say; it's all in the discovery. I'm not looking forward to it.

Carla quickly gets her to set the scene, confirming that she was Zimmer's girlfriend and that she had been there on the day in question. "I was hiding in the bedroom," Martinez says, "but the door was open a little bit, and I could see and hear everything."

"Did the defendant know you were there?"

She points to Kramer. "You mean him?"

Carla smiles. "Yes."

"No, he did not know I was there. Not until later. Thank God."

I object, and Avery sustains. He orders *Thank God* stricken from the record; judges clearly wield a lot of power.

Carla asks her to describe what happened, in her own words. I'm not sure who else's words Martinez might use, but she doesn't question the request.

"It was in the afternoon, and he knocked on the door. Pounded on it."

"You mean Mr. Kramer?"

Martinez nods. "Yes. Kenny went to the front door, and when he heard who it was, he told me to close the bedroom door. But I didn't close it all the way."

"Did Kenny let him in?"

Martinez nods. "Yeah. Kramer was angry; he started accusing Kenny of hitting on some underage girl. Said he molested her."

"What did Kenny say?" Carla asks.

"First, he said it wasn't true, but he used stronger words than that, you know? Then finally he said he did it but that no one could prove it."

"What happened next?"

"Kramer started beating him up. Kenny was a tough guy, but he didn't have a chance. It was awful. When Kramer left, I called 911."

"Did Kramer say anything to Zimmer before he left?" Carla asks, clearly leading the witness. I don't object, because one way or the other the answer will come in.

"Yes. He said that the next time he saw Kenny, he was going to kill him."

"Did you think he meant it?"

I object that Martinez could not possibly read my client's mind, and Avery sustains. Carla turns her over to me for cross. I have a lot of information at my disposal, both from the original assault case and from an interview that Laurie conducted with Martinez two weeks ago.

"Ms. Martinez, I'm sorry for your loss."

"What loss?"

"Kenny Zimmer. His death."

"I haven't been with him for two years," she says.

"Oh. What caused you to break up?"

"We were in Ohio. He was off doing something, and I was having a drink with a guy I met at a bar. An innocent drink; nothing was going on. Kenny comes in, and he starts pounding on the guy. I yelled at him to stop, and he hit me in the face. Nobody does that to me."

"So he was prone to violence?"

"Yeah."

"Did you ever know him to hold grudges?"

"Oh, yeah. You didn't want to get on Kenny's bad side."

"Would you say that Mr. Kramer got on Kenny's bad side when he beat him up?" I ask.

She laughs. "Yeah, you could say that."

"The question was whether you would say that," I point out.

"Yes."

"After you saw him beat Mr. Zimmer up, did Mr. Kramer discover that you were a witness to it?" I ask.

"Yes. He saw me through the opening in the door. I was scared."

"Did he do anything to you?"

"Just talked to me, that's all."

"Did he threaten you, because he knew you could testify against him for assault?" I ask.

"No. All he said was that I could do better than Kenny. That I'd be much better off without him."

"Was he right?"

"Oh, yeah. He sure was."

"The incident in Ohio where Zimmer hit you . . . you broke off the relationship after that?"

"Yes. I left that night and never looked back."

"Between the time Mr. Kramer beat up Zimmer and the time you left him . . . during that time, did Zimmer ever mention Mr. Kramer?"

She nods. "Oh, yeah. A lot. He hated him."

"To your knowledge, did Mr. Kramer ever contact Zimmer or attempt to do him harm?"

"No."

"No further questions."

As slow and painstaking as Carla is, the trial is going way too fast.

It won't be long before it's time to present the defense case, and the problem that presents is that we don't have a case worth presenting.

We are going to mount a self-defense theory of the killing, which is simultaneously true and not credible. The background stuff that we have been investigating, concerning Benjamin, Jeffries, Tina Bauer, and the rest of the crew, is for the most part inadmissible.

We need more to get it over that threshold. But unless the evidence fairy shows up with a basketful of exculpatory facts, I don't know where we are going to get them.

The only piece of truly concrete evidence that we have that unquestionably relates to this trial is Benjamin's fingerprint on the truck. There are other possible explanations for it being there, but it has led us to at least a partial understanding of what might be going on. Our ability to get that in front of a jury, or getting the jurors to believe us if we manage it, is very problematic.

The real difficulty is connecting the Craddock murder to all of this. I'm confident about that connection in my own mind, especially because of the break-in at Kramer's house, which removed the Craddock files. But I'm so far from being able to make the connection in a way that Judge Avery would find acceptable that I can't even convincingly demonstrate that Craddock was murdered.

I have lunch with Laurie and Hike at a restaurant near the courthouse, and across the room I see Pete, Carla, and two members of

Carla's team engaged in conversation over their own lunch. I wonder if Pete has mentioned to Carla that he discussed Eric Benjamin with me; if not, she might be surprised when I home in on it.

Pete is testifying this afternoon, and I haven't yet decided if I will bring up Benjamin or wait for our own case. I'll go with my instinct in the moment, which is what I usually do.

Pete, Carla, and the others leave before we do. They don't pass by our table, but close enough that Pete gives me the prefight Mike Tyson stare. We are simply not friends on the days that he testifies; he knows that I will try to take him apart, and his sole focus is on holding his own.

We've had some tussles in the past, and I would say it's come out fairly even. Pete is a solid, professional witness, and he has the added advantage of limiting his testimony to facts that he can back up.

Once Pete is on the stand, Carla spends more time than necessary taking him through his career path. She's establishing his credibility as a respected cop, and I'm about to object to the length of it, when she suddenly stops and moves to a discussion of why we are all here.

Pete is on the stand because he was in charge of the case, and he was also the arresting officer. It will be his job to tie the whole case together in a way the jury can understand. He is Carla's mid-trial closing argument.

"Captain Stanton, who notified you of the incident at the rest stop, which in turn made you go there?"

"There were actually two 911 calls. The first was made by John Paxos and the second by Ralph Brandenberger, the county animal control officer. Mr. Paxos's call was sufficient to generate the police presence."

"Were you the first on the scene?" she asks.

"I was not. Two other officers were there before me. They secured the scene, knowing I was on the way."

"How long was it from the time you arrived until you arrested the defendant?"

He thinks for a moment, pretending that this testimony is unrehearsed, when actually they've gone over every bit of it. "About six hours."

"Some people might consider that a rush to judgment," she says, her smile showing that she is not part of the "some people" she's talking about.

"Some people would be wrong."

"Can you tell us what went into your decision to make the arrest?"

"We had access to the security tape, which clearly showed Mr. Kramer arrive, enter the truck, and leave. We knew that Mr. Zimmer was alive before Mr. Kramer got on the truck, and—"

Carla interrupts. "How did you know that?"

"Well, the truck didn't drive itself there, and the tape shows no one getting on or off the truck after it arrived. But if somehow Mr. Zimmer was already dead, then an innocent person's actions would have been to call the police. Mr. Kramer didn't do that. I was also familiar with the history he had with the victim and his threat on his life."

"Anything else?" Carla asks.

"Yes, we sent officers to his house, and he had actually left a note for us, telling us we could find him at his criminal attorney's office."

"That's Mr. Carpenter?"

Pete nods. "Correct. So we authorized a search warrant. The defendant's gun was on the kitchen table, and we determined that it had recently been fired. All of that taken together gave me probable cause to make the arrest."

"Thank you, Captain Stanton. No further questions."

Pete has been very effective, and to leave him unchallenged is to let Carla end her case neatly tied up in a bow. I can't let that happen, so even though I was going to save everything for the defense case, I have to use part of the ammunition I have to make a statement now.

G ood afternoon, Captain Stanton," I say.
  "Good afternoon, Mr. Carpenter," Pete answers.

So far we are being polite as hell; it's practically a lovefest.

"Captain, when you are called to a murder scene like this, and when you investigate the case, you make assumptions, do you not?"

"I'm not sure what you mean."

"Which part didn't you understand?"

"In this context, I don't know what you're getting at when you say 'assumptions.' I go where the facts take me."

"First of all, just so we understand the ground rules here . . . it's not important that you know what I'm getting at. It's important that you truthfully answer the questions I ask. That's your only role here."

Carla objects that I'm being argumentative and harassing the witness, and while Avery overrules her, he tells me to be careful, that I am close to the line.

"Okay, to give you an obvious example by what I mean when I say you make assumptions, you boarded the truck and saw the victim lying dead with a bullet hole in his chest. That caused you to assume he was shot, even though you didn't see it happen. Correct?"

He nods. "Correct."

"Good," I say. "And since it was Mr. Kramer's gun that fired the fatal shot, and you saw on the tape that he boarded the truck, you assumed he was the killer, even though you didn't watch him do it. Correct?"

"Correct."

"Good. Now let's turn to some other assumptions you might have made. How did you assume that Mr. Kramer happened to be at the rest stop when Kenny Zimmer pulled up?"

"I can't say for sure, but they obviously had plans to meet."

"These mortal enemies said to each other, 'Hey, let's get together on your way through New Jersey. And since we both use bathrooms, let's do it at the rest stop.' Is that what you assume took place?"

"I don't know why they were there, but I know what happened once they got there."

"You do? Great! Tell us."

"Mr. Kramer shot and killed Mr. Zimmer," he says.

"I meant before that. Did he start firing immediately? Because according to the video, he didn't draw his gun before he boarded the truck."

"I don't know if he fired immediately."

"So that's an assumption that you can't make?"

"The point is that he fired."

"Did they argue first?"

"I don't know. Maybe they did."

"But you can't assume it one way or the other?"

"No. I wasn't there."

"Did Zimmer attack Mr. Kramer? Could Mr. Kramer have fired in self-defense, fearing for his life?"

"Zimmer was unarmed."

"That's an assumption you're willing to make?"

"It's not an assumption. There was no weapon on the truck, and it would have made no sense for Kramer to take it with him."

"Could there have been a third person on the truck, who took the weapon with him when he left?"

"No," he says.

"Assumption or fact?"

"Fact. The video does not show anyone leaving the truck, and when we arrived, there was no third person there."

"So let me give you a hypothetical, and tell me whether you think it's possible. Then we can discuss it further when I call you as a witness in the defense case."

"Fine."

"A third person, a suspected murderer in his own right, paid Zimmer a lot of money to try to kill Mr. Kramer. Zimmer then attacked Mr. Kramer with a weapon when he boarded the truck, but Mr. Kramer was able to fend him off and fired in self-defense. Then the third person, who was hidden throughout, exited the truck, with Mr. Zimmer's weapon, but without the video recording it. That's the hypothetical. Do you think it's possible?"

"I don't."

"Not even possible?" I ask.

"Not even possible."

"Then I look forward to talking to you later in the trial," I say. I tell Judge Avery that I am finished with this witness, subject to recall in the defense case.

What I have managed to do is present our entire theory of the case and get Pete to say it is absolutely not possible. Later, when I fill in the blanks and show that it is possible, my hope is that the jury will start to doubt him, and by extension Carla, and buy into reasonable doubt.

At this point, it's the only shot we have.

Once Pete leaves the stand, Carla rests the prosecution's case. So we're going to have to take that shot now.

In my dream, a cell phone rings, then rings again. It's a soft ring, and it doesn't sound like my ringtone, since mine is the *Godfather* theme music.

This sounds like Laurie's phone, and what I hear next sounds like Laurie's voice. "Marcus?" the voice asks. That jolts me completely awake; it is impossible to sleep through anything that includes Marcus.

I take a quick glance at the clock, which says 1:00 A.M. The chance of a call from Marcus at 1:00 A.M. being good news is too small to register as a percentage.

"What's going on?" I ask.

Laurie's response is to wave her hand at me in a gesture that simultaneously tells me to wait and be quiet. She has expressive hands. "Got it," she whispers to Marcus and hangs up.

Laurie turns to me and speaks in a calm, deliberate, very soft voice. "Andy, there is an intruder trying to come into our house. Very quietly go into Ricky's room. Make sure he is sleeping, and if he wakes up, make sure he does not come out."

"Is Marcus out there?"

"Andy, we don't have time to talk now."

There are a lot of questions I want to ask and a lot of things I think of doing. But I've learned enough to know that if there is a dangerous situation, and if Laurie and Marcus are in charge, I need to do what I'm told.

I get up and tiptoe down the hall to Ricky's room. Behind me as I leave the room, I see Laurie getting up as well. I don't know where she's going, but it has to be toward the danger, which scares the hell out of me.

I enter Ricky's bedroom and walk over to his bed. He's sound asleep, and the last thing I want to do is wake him. But I also want to go help Laurie, and I desperately want to know what is going on.

So I'm just standing here, frozen, with no idea what to do, mentally arguing with myself. And out there, where Laurie is, there is nothing but silence.

Finally, I come up with a plan. I leave Ricky's room but lock the door behind me. If he wakes up, and there is no sign that he's about to, he'll be forced to stay in his room. I'm okay with that; it's not like my being in there makes him any safer.

I walk down the hall toward the stairs, occasionally looking back to Ricky's closed door to make sure there is nothing happening there. I don't hear anything, which makes me extra cautious, because I don't want to blunder into anything and mess up whatever Laurie has planned. I still have no idea where Marcus is; I'd feel a lot better if he were standing next to me. Or better yet, next to Laurie.

Suddenly, I see a flash of light from the end of the hall and hear Laurie yell in as powerful a voice as she can manage, "Freeze! Drop your weapon and place your hands over your head!"

I move toward the railing from where I can see the light, downstairs. It's a powerful flashlight that Laurie is shining onto the face of an intruder who just entered through the back outside door, which leads into the corridor just outside the laundry room. I have no idea how he managed to circumvent our alarm system.

The intruder is grimacing in the glare, trying to get his eyes to adjust. I can't tell yet if I recognize who it is, because of the distance I am from him and the bright light shining on his face. But I can see that he is holding a large handgun.

"Now!" she yells. "Drop it now!"

But the man doesn't obey the command and drop the gun; instead, he raises it. And suddenly there is a deafening barrage, and he seems to explode.

He should have obeyed Laurie. I could have told him that's always the best choice to make.

"Laurie, are you all right?" I yell. She doesn't answer, but that's okay, because I see her heading for the intruder to make sure he's concluded his intruding career.

I go back to Ricky's room and unlock the door. I look in to see if he's still sleeping. He's not moving, so I go over and put my hand on his chest, to make sure he's breathing, and he is. How he slept through the chaos I have no idea, but he did.

I head toward the laundry room, and in addition to Laurie and the intruder's body, Marcus has joined the party. When I get there, I look down at the formerly living intruder.

It is Eric Benjamin.

"Ricky okay?" Laurie asks.

"He's sleeping."

Laurie walks away; I assume she's going to check on him. I go to the kitchen to get the phone so I can call Pete. But then I see that Laurie is already doing that. "I don't know who it is, Pete," she says.

"It's Eric Benjamin," I say.

Laurie relays that information to Pete and then says, "Thanks, Pete," before she hangs up. "He'll be right over," she says to me. Then she goes upstairs to check on Ricky.

Two patrol cars pull up before Pete gets here. They set up a perimeter around our house, now better known as the crime scene. Once Pete arrives and takes a quick look around, he calls in forensics and then the coroner. Pete takes Laurie and Marcus and me into the den to talk to us. "Proper procedure is for me to question you separately," he says. "But I think we can tolerate a little improper procedure right now."

Pete and I learn at the same time that Marcus has been secretly watching over me since Benjamin's threat, at Laurie's request. When he can't do so, he has assigned someone he works with to cover for him, though he doesn't say who that is, and it doesn't matter anyway.

I also learn that Benjamin was shot in both the front and back. Laurie was responsible for the front, Marcus the back. They had both seen him raise his weapon to fire, so both reacted.

"Why did he threaten you?" Pete asks me.

"Because I knew he was on the truck with Kenny Zimmer and,

therefore, had to be the one who ran off with the weapon after Zimmer was killed. And I suspected he killed John Craddock and Tina Bauer. And he knew I was going to expose him for all of it."

Pete just looks at me. He doesn't rebut or agree with what I've just said. He doesn't say a word.

He just looks at me.

Judge Avery delays the start of court this morning so we can meet with him in chambers. I'm not surprised; Benjamin's death is all over the papers and local newscasts this morning. Carla and one of her assistants join Hike and me.

"Well, Mr. Carpenter, I understand you had quite a night last night," Avery says. "You and your family are okay, I hope?"

"We are, thank you, Your Honor."

"I've brought you all in here to talk about the possible impact of these events on our trial. The jury has been instructed not to read or listen to anything about the trial, but we can't be sure they did not see coverage of this."

Carla says, "Even if they did, while it involved Mr. Carpenter, it should not have anything to do with our case. The deceased, Mr. Benjamin, is not relevant to the matter before you, Judge."

"Mr. Benjamin is very relevant to this matter, Judge, and that relevancy has just increased exponentially."

"Mr. Benjamin is part of your case?" Avery asks.

"Mr. Benjamin is a huge part of my case, and that was true even before last night."

Avery looks at me with a mixture of suspicion, skepticism, and annoyance. "I assume you will be able to back that up with facts rather than suppositions?"

"I look forward to it," I lie. What I don't say is that I hope every member of the jury heard all about Benjamin this morning and the way he met his death. I'm going to try to prove to them that he was a killer; what happened last night will only give my argument much more credibility.

"Do either of you have a motion to make regarding these latest events?" Avery asks.

He's giving Carla and me the opportunity to request a mistrial. I doubt he would grant it even if we did; he certainly would want to question the jurors individually first. But neither of us makes the request.

I actually think a mistrial would work substantially in our favor, as it would give us much more time to investigate Benjamin and his role in the Zimmer killing. But I'm not the one sitting in jail, and my client told me this morning in no uncertain terms that he wants to proceed.

So Avery sends us back in and starts off by renewing his instructions to the jury, this time telling them to avoid all news coverage, not just things that are connected to this trial.

Then he tells me to call my first witness, and I call George Davenport.

"Mr. Davenport, Kenny Zimmer worked for you?"

"He did. For only a month."

I've called Davenport to set up why Zimmer was on that truck in the first place and also to disabuse anyone of the notion that Zimmer was doing it to save the dogs. I don't want dog lovers on the jury to sympathize with him.

"How did you come to hire him?"

"He answered an online ad I posted on Craigslist."

"What were his responsibilities, specifically?" I ask.

Davenport relates how Zimmer would drive the truck down South, pick up dogs in shelters who were in danger of being euthanized, and bring them to rescue groups in New England.

"And that was the purpose of this trip?"

"Yes."

"Would Zimmer notify you where the dogs were going and other specific information about them?"

"He would, yes; he would email me," Davenport says.

"Did he for this trip?"

"No. I was surprised when I checked and discovered that he had not done so."

"Did I share with you my subsequent efforts to learn where the dogs on this trip were going?"

"You did. No groups were expecting them; Zimmer had failed to set that up. It is very strange; I can't imagine what he was planning to do with them."

"So in a number of ways, this trip was different from the others?"

"Apparently so. Yes."

Something Davenport has said triggers something in my mind, but for the moment, I can't access it. So instead I ask, "On this trip, other than not emailing you, did Mr. Zimmer behave in a way consistent with his responsibilities?"

"He did not," Davenport says.

"How much did Zimmer earn for making these trips?"

"A thousand dollars, plus thirty dollars a day for meals."

"What about hotels?"

"He slept on the truck." Obviously, the drivers must have slept in that padded room between the two sections of dog cages.

"Did you ever pay him $75,000?"

Davenport laughs at the suggestion. "No, sir."

Davenport has been a solid witness with no ax to grind. He hasn't been terribly important either way; all he did was set up work for us.

Carla asks a few perfunctory questions, but nothing of great consequence. She doesn't think that Davenport hurt her, and she is clearly right.

My next witness is Helena Saldana, a vice president at the bank where Zimmer kept his account. We learned from Sam's hacking that Zimmer received the wire transfer, so armed with that information, we obtained it through a legal subpoena.

After I establish who she is and that she has been called to discuss Kenny Zimmer's banking record, I ask, "Prior to two months ago, what was Mr. Zimmer's average account balance?"

"A little over $1,200," she says.

"And in the previous two years, what was the largest deposit he ever made?"

"Just under $3,000; it was made eighteen months ago."

"Was there an unusual deposit made six weeks before Mr. Zimmer's death?"

"Yes. He received a wire transfer in the amount of $75,000."

"Where did it come from?" I ask.

"The Cayman Islands."

"And who was the sender?"

"That's impossible to say. They have strict secrecy in their banking laws."

"So Zimmer received what was for him a huge amount of money from a secret source?"

"Yes."

"Thank you."

Nancy Pierce has been living in fear. Ever since the day that she had the paid liaison with Victor Andreson in the hotel room, her life has not been the same. The man that she knew as Manning had beaten her, and on his instructions, she had gone to the police and accused Andreson of the assault.

She was paid a great deal of money for doing so, and she had her eyes open going in. But what she hadn't fully realized was what an important businessman Andreson was or the chaos that would ensue.

And ever since, Andreson's lawyers had been coming at her in waves, dissecting her life and trying to prove that she was lying. It forced her into a shell, afraid to face each new day. She dreaded the time she would have to testify against Andreson at his trial; she was sure that those same lawyers would take her apart.

But all of those fears paled compared to what she was feeling now. It turns out that the man she knew as Manning was actually Eric Benjamin; she recognized him from his picture on TV and in the papers. And the reason his picture was there is that he had been killed.

Nancy remembered very clearly what Benjamin had said just before he left her hotel room that day. His words were, "There are some people that don't give a damn about you. I am the only reason you will stay alive."

Remembering those words, and knowing Benjamin was no longer

among the living, frightened her more than a hundred of Andreson's lawyers ever could.

Nancy decided in that moment that there was only one thing she could do.

She would tell the truth.

My first witness after lunch is Detective Linda Scalari. She was the officer that Pete had assigned to handle the fingerprinting of the storage rooms on the truck. I could have called a technician to testify, but I want to accomplish more than simply the identifying of the print.

Once I establish her role in this case, I hand her one of the discovery documents. "These are the names of the people whose prints you identified?"

"Yes."

"I direct you to the third name listed, E. Benjamin. Can you tell me what the *E* stands for?"

"Eric."

"Are you familiar with Eric Benjamin?"

"Very."

"Please tell the jury what you know about him."

Scalari talks about Benjamin in some detail, describing his work as a state cop, and then his losing that job because of accusations of theft and assault.

"Was he ever convicted of any of those charges?"

"He was never tried," she says. "The charges were dropped."

"Do you know why?"

She nods. "The main witness against him, Orlando Guadalupe, turned up dead."

I feign surprise. "Really? How? Pneumonia? Shot? Poisoned?"

"He was decapitated and dismembered."

Out of the corner of my eye, I can see the jury react and recoil, which is exactly the reaction I wanted.

I ask Scalari if Benjamin was a suspect in the Guadalupe murder, but Carla objects and Avery sustains. Then I ask, "Where is Mr. Benjamin today?"

Carla jumps up to object so quickly it's as if she saw a rattlesnake under her chair. Avery asks us to approach the bench.

Carla speaks first. "We just had a meeting about the possible negative effect of the awareness of Benjamin's death on the jury, and now Mr. Carpenter is bringing it out in testimony?"

"Your Honor," I say, "I have asked this witness to describe many aspects of Benjamin's life. Now I am asking her about his death. Just because that death is recent, and took place at my house, doesn't make it less relevant. In fact, Mr. Benjamin's attempt to invade the home of one of the lawyers in this case makes it far more relevant. The jury absolutely should consider it along with the other facts of the case."

"It could fatally prejudice the jury," Carla says.

I shake my head. "Your Honor, you didn't even think it was worth questioning the jurors to find out if they were aware of the events of last night. If you thought that awareness could 'fatally prejudice' them, you no doubt would have questioned them. I agreed with your ruling, and my bringing it out in testimony is completely consistent with that ruling."

I feel like I've successfully backed Judge Avery into a corner, but I also know that corners are not something that judges traditionally like being backed into.

He rules in my favor, but not totally. I am prohibited from having the witness mention that the murder happened at my house. I think that ruling is unfair, but I'm stuck with it.

Scalari is thus allowed to answer the question, and she says that "he is deceased; he was shot and killed."

"When?"

Again Carla objects, and again we approach. I explain that I am abiding by the judge's ruling and not having the witness mention my involvement, but that the timing is essential. I don't want the jury thinking Benjamin might have been killed before Zimmer.

My hope, of course, is that every member of the jury will disregard Judge Avery's instructions and do an online search for news of what happened last night.

Avery lets the timing of Benjamin's death in, and once Scalari says it, I turn her over to Carla.

Carla's focus is on the fingerprint. "Sergeant Scalari, you found Mr. Benjamin's print on the truck. When did he leave it there?"

"I have no idea."

"It could have been six months ago?"

"Possibly."

"Longer than that?"

"Could be."

"Do you know the circumstances under which he left them?"

"No."

"Thank you."

We're off to a decent start, in that the witnesses went pretty much according to plan. Unfortunately, the plan was not so great in the first place. The only significant fact brought in was Benjamin's print being found on the truck, and that is not exactly proof positive of his guilt.

I head home, only to discover Pete sitting in the den with Laurie. "Are you here to complain that I beat you up in court?"

"I wiped the floor with you," he says.

"Boys, boys . . . ," Laurie says.

"I didn't see your car outside," I say.

"I parked around the block and came in through the back."

That gets my interest; if Pete did that, he must have a damn good reason. "Okay. Let's hear it."

"You know the name Victor Andreson?" he asks.

"The doughnut guy? He cost us money."

"How?"

"Doesn't matter, believe me. Go on," I say.

"So you know the story? About how he beat up a hooker?"

I nod. "Yes. It was all over the news."

"Well, it turns out he didn't do it. He was with her, but someone else beat her up after he left. She agreed to it; she was paid fifty grand for letting it happen. Then she did what she was told and lied about Andreson."

"Let me guess," I say. "Benjamin beat her up."

Pete turns to Laurie and points to me. "He's not as dumb as he looks." Then, to me, "How did you know?"

"Because I see the pattern. They bring down executives that are crucial to their companies and find a way to profit from it. It happened with John Craddock, and I'll bet we find out it happened with Andreson."

"Maybe you are as dumb as you look," Pete says. "No matter how big a piece of garbage Benjamin was, Kramer killed Zimmer."

"In self-defense," I say.

"Yeah," Pete says, showing as much scorn as he can manage.

"Then why are you here? Why are you telling me this?"

"Because an agreement was made with the DA to keep this quiet for a while. They're afraid of Andreson and his lawyers. And I think Carla put her two cents in. They don't want you to use this to your advantage."

"So I repeat the question," I say. "Why are you telling me this?"

"I guess I believe in an even playing field."

"Wow. It took buying you about twenty thousand beers for you to turn decent on me. Now tell me what you've learned about why Benjamin tried to kill me."

"Wish I could. The feds took it over."

"When?"

"About thirty seconds after it happened. Givens was all over it. That's supposed to be off the record," he says. Then, "Like I give a shit."

We talk for a few more minutes, and then Pete says, "By the way, did you have your FBI friend run one of Zimmer's prints?" Laurie's and my friend Cindy Spodek is the number-two agent in the Boston office of the FBI, and I lean on her for a lot of favors.

"No. Why?"

He shrugs. "I got a call from the federal lab about the print. They got confused and thought I ran the print, because I was handling the Zimmer case. When I said I hadn't and asked who did, they clammed up."

"Beats me," I say.

Pete tells me he's heading down to Charlie's to listen to Vince complain about the Mets. I walk him to the back door, and as he's about to go out, I grab his arm and stop him.

"Pete, thanks for this."

"You're not going to kiss me good night, are you?"

"Not in this lifetime," I say. "But I do appreciate your doing this."

"It's the third time I helped you on this case."

I nod. "I know."

"If you tell anyone that I did, I will chop you up into little pieces and feed you to rabid coyotes."

"That's beautiful, Pete. I've never felt closer to you than I feel right now."

O nce Pete leaves, I place another call to Robbie Divine. I have no idea where he is; when one has his own private jet and pilot, one can be pretty mobile. It's 8:00 P.M. here in New Jersey; where Robbie is, it could be the middle of the night.

He answers the phone, sounding wide awake. But that's how he sounded last time, and I reached him at two thirty in the morning. "Again?" he asks.

"Did I wake you?"

"Wake me?" he asks. "You think I'm a hundred years old? It's mid-afternoon."

"Where are you?"

"Hawaii. Can we get to the point?"

"You do get around," I say.

"Rich people can do that. It's why you're always in New Jersey." Then, "The point?"

"The subject of today's call is Victor Andreson."

"He's a pig," Robbie says.

"You sound like Laurie. When he got arrested, his company's stock tanked. I lost a lot of money myself."

"You looking for a loan?"

"No, here's what I'm looking for. Suppose you knew, absolutely knew, that Andreson was going to be arrested and that his company's stock was going to crash, all before it happened. What would you do to profit from it? Sell short?" I'm using Freddie's terminology, even though I'm still unsure exactly what it means.

"No. Definitely not," he says.

"Then what?"

"I'd buy put options. That's by far the best way. But if you're going to get into the company-tanking business, you'd be better off making it more than one."

"Why?"

"Because everything is regulated and watched. If you suddenly loaded up on puts on a specific stock, and then it went way down, regulators would be up your ass."

"I'd rather not have regulators up my ass," I say.

"Smart man."

"By the way, what exactly are put options?"

"Google it."

"Thanks. I will."

So I hang up and I google *put options*, and it doesn't surprise me that Robbie is right.

At this point, I'm confident in my assessment of what is going on. Benjamin has been instrumental in bringing down two extraordinarily successful businessmen who were integral to their companies' success.

When they were eliminated, Craddock murdered and Andreson arrested, their companies predictably took a nosedive. And I believe Benjamin and his coconspirators were there to profit from it.

If I'm correct, then Kramer was a bit player in all this. The conspirators must have been afraid that he was about to figure out their scheme while investigating the Craddock death. It feels like an overreaction; they had already made their profit by then. To pay Zimmer $75,000 and to go to all this trouble, there must be something more, something that I'm missing.

Something more to come.

I call Sam and tell him I have two daunting jobs for the Bubalah Brigade. One is to search the last six months and find every company that suffered a precipitous drop in stock price or value. Then try to determine if the cause of it was the loss of an executive who was integral to the company.

It's a huge job, but fortunately one made a bit easier due to the fact that the stock market has had a mostly steady rise during that time. Therefore, there shouldn't be that many companies that collapsed so completely.

Sam takes the task in stride, expressing confidence that they can handle it. The other assignment, however, is one he doesn't think they can pull off. I've asked him to find out who held put options on Victor's Donuts when Andreson was arrested.

"Andy, not only are the stock exchanges almost impossible to hack, but they wouldn't even have the information. The names of the holders of the options would be at the brokerages that purchased them for their clients. We have no way of even knowing which brokerages are the ones we are looking for.

"And even if we did know, and if we could break into them, they could be held in the names of dummy companies set up for this purpose. I'm sorry; it's just not going to happen."

"I understand," I say, and then just before I hang up, I think of one more thing to ask. "Sam, you told me that Hilda had done a deep dive on Benjamin. Did that include credit card records?"

"Of course."

"Can you tell me if he traveled anywhere? Airline tickets, rental cars? I'm thinking primarily the Caymans, but it could be anywhere. I just want as much information on him as I can get."

"That's an easy one; I'll get back to you real soon. The companies whose stock crashed might take a little longer, maybe until tomorrow."

"Thanks, Sam. And thank the brigade for me."

My last call is to FBI agent Jeffrey Givens. We agreed to share information, and as long as nothing I say jeopardizes my client's position, I want to keep the relationship going. He hasn't provided any help so far, but you never know.

He gets on the phone right away, which is already a sign of worry, if not desperation. Usually FBI agents take longer to reach on the phone than a human at the DMV.

"What have you got, Andy?"

Calling me Andy is another sign of anxiety and need on his part. He's trying to act like we're buddies in the hope that maybe I'll be more forthcoming. One thing we are not is buddies.

"I assume you are aware that Mr. Benjamin has left this earth?"

"Tell me something that's not in the papers."

"I will do that," I say, "secure in the knowledge that you will reciprocate. I think you should lean on a guy named Greg Hepner. He's the head of a company called Sky Robotics."

"Why?"

"Because what I think Benjamin was doing, and probably Jeffries as well, was seeing to it that key executives at companies got eliminated, and then profiting when those companies collapsed. It happened with John Craddock, who they murdered, and Victor Andreson, who they framed."

"Where does Hepner fit in?"

"His company is a direct competitor of Craddock's company. He's even poached some employees after Craddock died. And Sky Robotics then took off in an IPO. We're talking more than a billion dollars."

Givens pauses for a few moments and then says, "Interesting. Anything else?"

"You sure you want to go out on a limb like that?" I ask. "Now what have you got for me?"

"Nothing, I'm afraid."

"Thus ends the Carpenter-Givens information pact."

"What do you want?"

"Well, for one thing, I want to know what you've learned about Jeffries. For another, I want to know why you are unimpressed with the information I've just given you."

"Fair enough," he says. "We've learned very little about Jeffries. We know there were large sums of money going into and out of the Caymans, under his direction. We don't know the details yet, other than that some went to procure the weapons I told you about. And while I think your theory is interesting, and maybe even accurate, what is going on is much bigger than that. And much more dangerous."

"Okay," I say. "The pact has been restored."

"Good. I am reachable 24-7."

Getting Benjamin's name before the jury was a big step for us. The real key, however, would be getting them to hear my theory of the case. That is going to be up to Judge Avery, and it will have to wait until we are finished with the self-defense portion.

My next witness is William Shepherd, a phone company employee who manages the local billing department. We've subpoenaed our own client's phone records, mainly because we've already seen them through the magic of Sam Willis and the Bubalah Brigade.

I use Shepherd to testify about the records and get him to say that there is no record of Kramer having called any number registered to Kenny Zimmer. Then I call his attention to the two calls made to Kramer from Little Rock and northern Virginia.

"Who owns the phone that made those calls?" I ask.

He shrugs. "I'm afraid I can't tell you that. It's a phone purchased at a convenience store without a contract. It utilizes our service system, but as far as our company is concerned, the owner remains anonymous."

"So there were two calls from that phone, the first from Little Rock and then two days later from northern Virginia," is how I recap it. "Is there any evidence that Mr. Kramer called that phone?"

"No," Shepherd says. "He did not."

Carla comes right to the point in her cross. "Mr. Shepherd, these calls from Little Rock and Virginia, do you have any idea who made them?"

"No, I don't."

"Do you know what was said in those calls?"

"I do not."

"Thank you."

Carla walks back to the prosecution table shaking her head slightly, as if disgusted with the nonsense she has to put up with.

Next, I call Betty Stuart, the elderly owner of the convenience store where the phone was purchased. We flew her up here, and Laurie took her to dinner last night. Laurie said she laughed all night and that Betty is hilarious and an all-around terrific lady.

That may be true, but once Betty is on the stand, she's all business. She has brought records demonstrating that the phone was purchased in her store and that she remembers it well. She identifies Zimmer through a photograph and identifies the truck that he was driving, also through a photograph.

"He just pulled in and left that truck in the middle of the parking lot. No one could get in or out. When I told him that, he just said that he'd be gone as soon as he got the phone."

"How did he pay for it?"

"Cash," she says. "A hundred-dollar bill. I looked that bill over carefully, I can tell you that. He looked like the type to try to pass a fake."

The final witness in the self-defense portion of our case is a recall of Pete Stanton. I indirectly promised the jury a great deal when I cross-examined him during the prosecution's case, and I need to deliver on it. I had presented Pete a hypothetical of what might have happened that day at the rest stop, and he responded that it was not possible.

I need to show the opposite.

Pete takes the stand and says yes when Judge Avery asks him if he understands that he's still under oath.

"Welcome back, Captain Stanton."

He smiles. "My pleasure, Mr. Carpenter."

"Last time you were here, you said that you had no idea how it came to be that Mr. Kramer was at the rest stop at the same time Mr. Zimmer was."

"Right."

"Were you in the court when Betty Stuart testified that Zimmer purchased the phone that called Mr. Kramer twice?"

"I was."

"And did you also hear the previous testimony that Mr. Kramer never called that phone?"

"Yes."

"Has that changed your view as to who instigated the meeting?"

He shakes his head. "Not with any certainty, no. There could have been previous calls, other phones could have been used; I don't have enough information yet."

"Perhaps you could have conducted an investigation that would have provided that information."

Carla objects before Pete can respond, and Avery overrules her. Pete doesn't answer, because I hadn't really asked a question. It was more of a statement.

"In my hypothetical to you, I mentioned the possibility that Mr. Zimmer had wielded a weapon, causing Mr. Kramer to shoot him in self-defense. You said that was not possible, because no weapon was found. Do you remember that?"

"Yes."

"And I raised the possibility that there might have been a third person on the truck, who removed the weapon. You also said that was not possible, because the video would have shown that person. Do you recall that as well?"

"I do."

I introduce as evidence the tape that the security camera took of me at the rest stop two days after the murder. I had requested it from Pete, but I doubt he ever saw it.

It shows me arriving and boarding the truck. Seven very long minutes go by where it shows absolutely nothing else except the truck, sitting there silently. It is a film unlikely to win a Golden Globe.

Then I suddenly come into frame, walking along the ramp that the cars would take coming in from the highway. The gallery, and I think the jury, start to murmur among themselves, surprised to see me, since they thought I was still on the truck.

I walk to the truck, turn to the camera, and wave. It is an extraordinary performance; one of my greatest roles.

Once the tape has finished, I turn back toward Pete. "So as you saw, I was on the truck, then got off the truck and reappeared without the camera picking up any of it."

"Yes."

"Do you know how I did it?" I ask.

"You must have gone out the back of the truck and used the truck to shield you from the camera as you went to the highway."

"Exactly. So is it possible that the truck was deliberately parked in that strange fashion so that it would block the camera when someone left the truck?"

"You don't know that," he says.

"I asked if it was possible that someone else could have done exactly what I did."

"There is no evidence to support your view."

"Are you having trouble understanding the question? Should I have the court reporter read it back? I asked if it was possible. My view has nothing to do with it."

"It's possible," he acknowledges, "but there is no evidence to support it."

"Evidence? You mean like a fingerprint?"

"There is no telling when Benjamin was on that truck."

"Captain, last time you were on the stand, I gave you a hypothetical, and you said it wasn't possible. Now you admit that it is. So let me try another hypothetical, adding some specifics that we've learned. Eric Benjamin, or some people he worked for, paid Kenny Zimmer $75,000 to lure Mr. Kramer onto that truck. Benjamin was on the truck as well, hiding and accidentally leaving his fingerprint. Zimmer attacked Mr. Kramer with a knife, but Mr. Kramer was able to avoid it and shot and killed him in self-defense. Benjamin was fine with that, because he knew there was another way to get rid of Kramer, by framing him for murder. So he took the knife and exited the truck, knowing that the position of the truck would allow him to avoid the security cameras. Is that possible?"

Pete thinks for a while and finally says, "It is possible, but not reasonable."

Tomorrow will be the key day of the trial. We need Judge Avery to rule in our favor, to allow the jury to hear our theory of the case.

Of course, even if he does, it doesn't mean that we'll win. The jury could hear everything we have to say and still vote to convict Kramer.

It's like a field goal kicker trying a long field goal on the last play of regulation, with his team down three points. If he makes it, they remain alive and continue to play in overtime. If he misses, they lose. So all he is kicking for is to give his team a chance, which is why the situation is similar. We just want Judge Avery to give us a chance.

I ask Hike how he thinks we should go about it. We could ask for a meeting in chambers or just go ahead and start presenting the evidence, knowing that Carla will object and Avery will decide in the moment.

"I would go for the meeting in chambers," Hike says. "It's an important issue, and Avery will be pissed if he doesn't have a chance to rule on it."

"If we just start calling witnesses without calling attention to the new approach, it would signal that we don't think there's an admissibility question," I say. "Getting Benjamin's print into evidence opens the door."

"Judge Avery is in control of the door, and if he feels like you're trying to push him around, he'll keep it closed."

"I need to think about it," I say. "Either way, you think he'll let it in?"

"No," Hike says.

What a surprise.

Sam calls with news about Benjamin's potential travel, as determined by his credit card purchases. "Sorry it took so long," Sam says. "The guy has six credit cards and then another three registered to his bullshit security firm."

"No problem. What did you find out?" I'm hoping he took some trips to the Caymans. That wouldn't prove anything, but it would tie him closer to Jeffries, which I could use in front of the jury.

"Not much. Definitely no long trips, at least not ones where he used his credit card. He did drive to South Jersey, though. Based on his gas, hotel, and restaurant charges, he drove down there, stayed overnight, and then left the next morning."

"Where did he go?"

"Chesterfield, New Jersey. It's mostly farmland down there. He stayed in a Holiday Inn Express; I wouldn't think it would be up to his standards."

"Send me the address of the hotel and any restaurants he went to down there, please."

"Will do."

Any move that Benjamin made is interesting to me, though obviously his reason for going to Chesterfield could have been completely benign. He could have been visiting his aunt Doris.

For now, I call George Davenport and ask him if he's ever heard of Chesterfield, New Jersey.

"No, I don't think so. Where is it?"

"South Jersey," I say.

"Why do you ask?"

I'm not a big fan of answering questions; I prefer to ask them. So I ignore his and ask, "Do you know if by any chance that was a drop-off point for dogs? Might Zimmer have stopped there?"

"I can't imagine that he did. His first drop-off was always in Connecticut. No reason to have gone that far off the highway."

I thank him and get off the phone. Maybe I'll pursue the Chesterfield angle or maybe I won't; it depends how desperate I am as the trial proceeds.

By the time I get home from court, Ricky and Laurie have had dinner. She's saved some for me, and they are nice enough to sit with me while I eat. I am looking forward to getting back to a normal life. Murder trials and normal life are two mutually exclusive concepts.

Ricky joins me on the evening walk with Tara and Sebastian. I'm feeling fairly safe now that Benjamin is dead, and for all I know, Laurie still has Marcus following me, providing protection. One can only see Marcus when he wants to be seen.

So we talk about the start of school, and Ricky's teacher, and a girl Ricky sort of likes named Leslie. They're the things I would already know if I wasn't lost in my own world.

Ricky thinks that Leslie is kind of cute because she has a ponytail, but he doesn't really talk to her much. I suggest that he strike up a conversation with her sometime, and he says, "Nah." Then he says that he might text her. He doesn't have a cell phone, so I don't know how he can do that. Actually, I don't think I want to know.

When we get home, I call Willie to ask how the dogs from the truck are doing. I haven't been able to get over to the foundation much, which leaves me constantly feeling guilty.

Sondra answers and in answer to my question says, "They're doing great, Andy. We've placed seven of them and have a bunch of people coming in tomorrow."

"How's Wiggy?" Wiggy is the golden with the puppies.

"Fantastic. Don't tell him I told you, but I think Willie wants to keep her. He thinks Cash wants a friend."

Cash is Willie's Lab mix. We found him stray the day he won his big lawsuit, hence the name. "That would be great."

"The problem is there's another dog, I think it's a pit bull mix, that Willie wants also. It could start getting crowded at our house."

"You'll work it out."

"I'm not so sure. It's pretty hard to say no to Willie, especially when dogs are concerned."

I hope Willie takes them both. I've had my eye on Wiggy, but Tara would probably be annoyed if I brought home another golden.

I settle into the den to prepare for tomorrow's trial day, but thinking about the dogs reminds me of something that continues to gnaw at me. If Zimmer was planning on luring Kramer to the truck to kill him, and if he hadn't contacted any rescue groups about taking the dogs, then what the hell were the dogs doing on the truck? Why pick them up and bring them all the way to New Jersey?

While it's unlikely to have anything to do with our case, it's a question that I'd love to know the answer to. And when this is all over, I'm going to find that answer, even if I have to visit every shelter and rescue group in New England.

Your Honor, before we call our next witness, may we approach the bench?"

Judge Avery calls us up and leans down to converse with Carla and me. I've decided to do it this way, in a sidebar, in effect splitting the difference between Hike's idea of an in-chambers conference and my idea of just winging it.

This seems like it's less of a big deal, though I'm sure Carla will have a stroke.

"Your Honor, we are about to begin a new phase of our case, and I wanted you to be aware of it in advance."

"What might that be?" he asks, clearly wary of what I might be doing.

"I believe that Eric Benjamin was part of a conspiracy that, among many other criminal acts, attempted the murder of David Kramer. Kenny Zimmer was paid to perform the act, but that was thwarted when Mr. Kramer killed him in self-defense. Since the purpose was simply to remove Mr. Kramer, Benjamin framed Mr. Kramer for the murder. A plan B, as it were."

"Your Honor, this isn't going off on a tangent, it's going off to another planet," Carla says.

"In your scenario, who fired the shot that killed Zimmer?" Judge Avery asks.

"My client did; we have never disputed that. But it was in self-defense. And if you let me introduce my theory, I believe it is far more credible than the theory that Mr. Kramer boarded that truck with the intent to kill. The jury will be swimming in reasonable doubt."

Not surprisingly, Carla is not convinced. "Your Honor, he is just trying to confuse the jury. If Eric Benjamin were alive, and he committed so many criminal acts, then he would be on trial himself . . . in another courtroom. Because he is separate and distinct from this case."

"Your Honor," I say, "how can he not be a relevant actor in this trial if his fingerprint was found at the murder scene?"

"I'll allow it for now," the judge says, probably worried about a future appeals court reviewing his actions if he didn't allow it. "But you will be on a short leash."

He doesn't get the irony of talking about a leash when we're discussing a truckload of dogs, and I'm not about to laugh at him for it.

I give Hike a slight nod to show that we won the point as I head back to the defense table. "The defense calls Christine Craddock."

The doors at the back of the courtroom open, and Christine Craddock comes in. She's in her wheelchair, and she comes all the way up to the bench. "You may sit there rather than the witness stand, if that's your preference," Judge Avery says graciously.

"Thank you," Christine says. This is a woman who lends dignity to any room she enters, certainly including this one.

The bailiff comes over and sets up the witness microphone on a small stand next to her so that she can talk into it. She thanks him and turns to face me as I approach.

"Mrs. Craddock, you were married to John Craddock?"

"Yes."

"And he was the head of a company called Roboton?"

"Yes."

"Would it be fair to say that your husband earned a great deal of money and that he left a substantial inheritance?"

"One hundred and fourteen million dollars. Plus ninety percent of the company."

"Have you determined the value of the company?"

"No, but it is far less than one might expect. John was a genius in robotics; he was the company. Unfortunately, it is apparently crumbling in his absence."

I lead her into her hiring of Dave Kramer as an investigator to confirm that her husband was cheating on her. "You suspected that he was?"

She nods. "I had very little doubt about it, and Mr. Kramer confirmed it in short order."

"Did that end the work he was doing for you?"

"For the time being . . . as it turned out a very short time. It wasn't long after that that John was killed."

She relates the circumstances of the death, emphasizing John's love of nature and his respect for its dangers. "There was no way John could have had that kind of accident. I believed that he was murdered, and I believe it now. I employed Mr. Kramer for a second time, to investigate this possibility."

"What did he find?"

"I don't know. Before he could complete his work, he was arrested."

Carla's questioning is quick and dismissive, as if to demonstrate that this is just a distraction and not worth paying much attention to.

"Mrs. Craddock, I am sorry for your loss."

"Thank you."

"Prior to your being contacted or being involved in this trial, had you ever heard the name Eric Benjamin?"

"No."

"Kenny Zimmer?"

"No."

"You've said that you believe your husband was murdered. Do you have any evidence of that?"

"No."

"Any idea who might have done it?"

"No."

"Thank you."

etective Doug Cameron is the guy that Pete assigned to investigate the Tina Bauer disappearance. I start him off by getting him to tell the jury that Tina Bauer went missing on the same day that John Craddock died. Then I ask him if there was any connection between the two people.

"Yes, Tina Bauer and John Craddock were having an affair."

"You've confirmed that through your own investigation?"

"I have, in a number of different ways."

"Was she with him on the day that he died?"

"Yes, the evidence indicates she was. Two other hikers saw them arrive at the entrance to the trail. They have both made positive identifications."

"In your investigation, have you talked to anyone who has reported seeing Tina Bauer since that day?"

"No."

"Have her credit cards or phone been used?"

"They have not," he says.

"So there has been no trace of her at all?"

"Correct."

"Detective Cameron, did you examine Tina Bauer's phone records in the weeks before her death?"

He nods. "I did."

"Did the name Eric Benjamin come up in connection with that?"

"Yes. She received two calls from Mr. Benjamin."

"What is the status of your Tina Bauer investigation today?" I ask.

"She is a missing person and also a person of interest in the death of John Craddock."

"You say 'death of John Craddock.' Do you think Mr. Craddock died from an accidental fall?"

"You want my personal opinion?" he asks.

"Yes, please."

"I do not believe he died of an accidental fall. I believe he was murdered."

"And Tina Bauer . . . where is she today? Your personal opinion."

"I think that the most likely scenario is that she was a participant in the crime, and then her partner turned on her. It is also possible, but less likely, that she was murdered along with Mr. Craddock."

"Why do you think it more likely that she was a participant?" I ask.

"Because of the phone calls from Benjamin. My theory is that she lured Craddock to that spot at Benjamin's direction. She may not have realized that the purpose was to murder him, but that's the way it played out."

I thank him and turn him over to Carla.

"Detective Cameron, the focus of your investigation has been the disappearance of Tina Bauer?"

"Yes."

"You said it was likely that she was a participant in the murder because of phone calls from Mr. Benjamin."

"Yes."

"Do you have any evidence of what was discussed?"

"I do not."

"Isn't a phone call a weak basis to accuse someone of murder?"

"I was asked for my theory," he says.

"Did she receive calls from other people?"

"Of course."

"Does that make those other people who called her murderers also?" Carla asks, raising her voice.

"Of course not."

"Detective, do you have any evidence that Tina Bauer even knew Kenny Zimmer?"

"No."

"Did she know David Kramer?"

"Not to my knowledge."

"Did you, in your investigation, turn up any evidence at all between Tina Bauer and the issue that this jury is here to resolve?"

"I did not."

"Thank you."

We're off this afternoon because the judge has to deal with some unrelated matters. It was a decent day for us, but I am afraid I'm dealing with a confused jury. They're here to make a judgment about Dave Kramer, and they are hearing about something that seems to have nothing to do with him.

Judge Avery has allowed me a lot of leeway so far, but I'm going to need more time and space to make the jury understand what the hell is going on.

After lunch, I call Givens of the FBI to find out if he followed my advice and put pressure on Greg Hepner, who I believed profited from Craddock's murder.

Once again, he gets on the phone immediately, and when he hears what I want, he says, "We did. He lawyered up immediately. The guy is definitely dirty, and he's scared."

"So what's your next step?"

"We're looking into his IPO money." Then, "You have anything for me?"

"No," I say.

"So why am I talking to you?"

"Because I'm charming."

"Call me when you have something," he says and hangs up.

Is it possible I'm not as charming as I'd thought?

Nancy Pierce definitely does not want to be here. She admitted as much to Laurie when they went over her upcoming testimony, but she's stuck, since we subpoenaed her. And since she's already told the story to law enforcement, she can't lie about it now.

"Ms. Pierce, what is your occupation?"

"I am . . . I was . . . an escort."

"You're retired?" I ask.

She nods. "Permanently."

"As an escort, what were your job responsibilities?"

"I would go on dates and see to it that those dates were satisfied."

"Did that satisfaction include sexual satisfaction?"

"Frequently."

"When did you meet Victor Andreson, the founder and chief executive of Victor's Donuts?"

Carla stands up, looking exasperated. "Your Honor, may we approach?"

Avery okays it, and we head up for another sidebar. "Your Honor," Carla says, "are we going to litigate every crime ever committed by anyone? When will we get to the Kennedy assassination? What does this all have to do with the case we are trying?"

Avery turns to me. "Mr. Carpenter, it is explanation time."

I nod my agreement. "Your Honor, Mr. Benjamin was involved in a conspiracy to remove certain heads of companies through criminal means. They chose executives whose departures would do irreparable harm to their companies, and they were prepared to profit from it. One of Mr. Benjamin's coconspirators has already been killed in the Cayman Islands to preserve their secret."

Judge Avery says, "Interesting. What does that have to do with our trial?"

"Mr. Kramer was investigating the murder of John Craddock. He was close to exposing it, so they put him out of commission to ensure he would be unable to."

"You can prove this?"

I've got to be careful here. "I can come close enough to convince the jury, if you'll let me. I can cite rulings from various appeals courts to support my position."

I hope he doesn't ask me to cite those cases, because I made that part up. I raised the appeals court issue because I know he doesn't want to be overturned down the road.

Carla says, "Your Honor, I renew my objection. We are here because of the murder of Kenny Zimmer, and Mr. Carpenter has the jury listening to testimony about hookers and doughnuts."

Avery thinks for a few moments and then says, "Proceed, Mr. Carpenter."

I resume questioning Pierce regarding her interaction with Victor Andreson. She describes him coming to the hotel room and their having sex.

"And then he left? Did he harm you in any way?"

She shakes her head. "No."

"What happened after he left?"

"Another man came to my room. We had planned it that way."

"Who was the other man?"

"Eric Benjamin."

"Did he harm you in any way?"

"Yes." She proceeds to describe how Benjamin beat her and how she then went to the police and accused Andreson of doing it.

"Why did you agree to it?"

"He paid me $50,000."

"So you lied to the police?"

She nods. "Yes."

"What made you finally decide to tell the truth?"

"I saw on television that Benjamin was killed. He had told me only he could protect me from the people he was working with. So I got scared." Then, "I'm still scared."

Carla starts her cross with, "Ms. Pierce, you've already lied once about the facts you are testifying about today?"

"Yes."

"Even though you knew a man might go to prison because of your lies?"

"Yes."

"But we should believe you now?"

"I'm telling the truth now."

"So you say."

I object, and Avery sustains.

Carla once again is limited in how much she can challenge what these witnesses are saying, because they happen to be telling the truth. Therefore, the rest of her cross-examination is limited to pointing out that Pierce has absolutely no knowledge of anything having to do with the Kenny Zimmer murder.

The trial has fallen into a pattern. I think I am effectively driving home the point that Eric Benjamin was a bad guy who was involved in a criminal conspiracy. I think I could get the jury to convict him of murder, or if not that, some form of fraud. I certainly could nail him for the assault on Nancy Pierce.

The problem, of course, is that this judge and jury are not here to judge Eric Benjamin. And even if they convicted him, it would be tough to give him the death penalty, because he's already dead.

Carla points this all out at every opportunity she has, and she makes effective points in the process. No matter how bad an actor Benjamin was, she points out, it has little to do with Zimmer and Kramer.

The only concrete link I have between Benjamin and the Zimmer killing is the fingerprint in the truck. I've used that as a jumping-off point to sell the jury on a completely different theory of the case, and I'm not sure that they have the slightest idea what I'm talking about.

I don't have any choice but to continue down this path, of course, with no guarantee that I'm making progress defending Dave Kramer. But the one key decision that's facing me is whether or not Kramer should testify in his own defense.

It's the most important decision for a defense attorney in every trial, but it's not one that I feel I can make on my own. My view is that a defendant always makes that final call; if he's going to be convicted without speaking up for himself, that has to be his choice.

I always strongly advise the client on my point of view, and I can't remember the last time I advised that he testify. Exposing him to cross-examination is generally an invitation to disaster. But this time may be the exception; it was only Zimmer, Benjamin, and Kramer on that truck, so Kramer is the only person left alive who knows without a doubt what happened. It might be effective for him to tell what he experienced to the jury.

I discuss it with him, and his inclination is to testify. I apprise him of the dangers, and he agrees with me that we should wait until the time comes to make that final decision.

My next witness is Sarah Maurer, a financial analyst for a large brokerage firm specializing in tech stocks. Within that area, her focus is on robotics, and she is considered the most knowledgeable in that field.

I take her through her credentials, which are considerable. She's the go-to person for business media when it comes to this industry, and if the jury watches CNBC, they will no doubt recognize her.

"Ms. Maurer, what was the effect on Roboton when John Craddock was killed?"

Carla objects, stating correctly that there has been no determination that Craddock was "killed" and that his death is still officially considered accidental.

Judge Avery sustains, and I rephrase the question. "Ms. Maurer, what was the effect on Roboton when John Craddock, an experienced hiker, inexplicably fell off a mountain?"

Carla objects again, and Avery warns me. I rephrase again, and finally Maurer gets to answer. "It was devastating for the company. Craddock was brilliant, and he was certainly the driving force behind Roboton. It was literally a case of the body dying when the head was cut off."

"Are they still in business?"

"Technically, yes. But many of their top people have left, and they have lost most of their contracts."

"Will the company recover?" I ask.

"Highly unlikely."

"Is robotics a zero-sum game?" I ask. "By that, I mean if one company is hurt, does another thrive?"

"I'm not sure I'd characterize it exactly that way, but certainly the failure of one company, or the loss of one executive, does not mean the field is going away. So, yes, other companies will invariably pick up the slack."

"In this particular case, has any one company seemed to benefit more than any other?" I ask.

"Yes. The clearest victor, if you will, is Sky Robotics. They are a direct competitor to Roboton; they are developing similar products. They were having their initial public offering just a few weeks after Mr. Craddock's death. Almost immediately they hired two of Roboton's top people."

"What was the financial effect?"

She thinks for a few moments. "Well, most people thought the IPO would be priced at fifteen dollars a share. After all of this happened, the price went to twenty-seven dollars. So the value of the company increased by well over a billion dollars."

"Who realized that gain?"

"Well, forty percent would have gone to the company founder, Gregory Hepner. The rest would have gone to his investors."

"And I had asked you to look into who those investors might be. Did you do that?"

"I haven't been able to figure that out yet. Another forty percent are mostly companies that are rather opaque; they seem to have been designed to shield the principals. A number of them are foreign based."

Next, I turn the conversation to Victor Andreson. I ask her the same questions about the effect on his company.

She says, "The stock dropped almost twenty-five percent when the arrest was announced and more details emerged."

"Did other companies profit by the fall?"

"Not really," she says. "The field is fairly spread out with other large players. If there was an impact on their stock prices, it was minimal."

"So did anyone profit from Mr. Andreson's fall from grace?" I ask.

She nods. "Oh, yes. There were a number of outstanding put options at that time; actually, an unusually high number."

I get her to give a brief explanation of put options, and she does so in a clear and concise manner. The main point, that the jurors could not miss, is that people who buy puts can make a lot of money when a stock goes down.

"And did you find out who bought these puts?"

"Again, much of it was opaque, and many of the companies were foreign."

"Is all this unusual?" I ask.

"In my experience, to this level, yes."

"How much could the holders of these puts have made with the drop of the stock?"

"Hard to figure, but definitely in excess of $250 million. Possibly more."

"Do they still have the puts?"

She shakes her head. "No, they have all been exercised. The holders are long since gone."

"So just to recap, there are people who earned huge sums of money because of the death of John Craddock and the downfall of Victor Andreson?"

"Absolutely."

I turn the witness over to Carla, who starts off with, "Ms. Maurer, were you paid to be here today?"

"Yes."

"Just like you were paid for other times you have testified?"

"Yes."

"And you have always testified for the defense?"

"Except for a couple of times. But mostly for the defense, yes."

"What do you charge for your role as witness?" Carla asks, deliberately not using the traditional word *expert* before *witness.*

"My standard rate is $10,000."

"So you earned $10,000 for"—she looks at her watch—"forty minutes?"

Here it comes . . .

"No, I charged one hundred dollars in this case."

Carla looks like she was hit by a verbal truck. "Why?"

"Because the idea that stock prices can be manipulated or companies destroyed through violence is so horrible that I want to make sure it is exposed."

Kaboom. Carla made the classic mistake of asking a question she didn't know the answer to.

"Very noble," Carla says. "I think it's awful as well; it just has nothing to do with this case."

I object, and Avery reprimands her strongly for giving that unsolicited opinion.

The rest of Carla's cross focuses on Maurer having no idea as to whether the people who made all the money had anything to do with Kenny Zimmer's death. But basically, she just wants to get Maurer off the stand as fast as possible.

I definitely got my hundred dollars' worth.

Dave Kramer has decided to testify.

I advised him against it, but I don't feel nearly as strongly about it as I usually do. He's an experienced witness from his time as a police officer, and not only does he have a story to tell, but he's really the only one who can tell it.

He will be our final witness, and since it won't be until Monday, we have time to prepare. I haven't officially told the court that he will testify, so Carla will have to prepare for a cross-examination over the weekend. Hopefully she won't work too hard on it, since she knows how rarely defendants testify in their own defense.

Hike and I are going to spend the day on Sunday at the jail going over his testimony. It's fair to say I'm not looking forward to it, though surrounded by all that gray misery should be a fun time for Hike.

We have nothing planned for Saturday, though, so during breakfast, I say to Laurie and Ricky, "I've got a great idea. Let's go to Chesterfield."

"The old cigarette?" Laurie asks. "What are you talking about?"

"It's in New Jersey; we can have a fun day. There's lots to do there. There are roads, and farms, and grass, and stuff."

Ricky chimes in. "Huh?"

"Sounds like a dream vacation," Laurie says. "It wouldn't happen to be connected to the case, would it?"

"Yes, but that's the beauty of it. Everything we spend will be tax deductible."

"Oh, boy," she says. "But Ricky is spending the day at Will Rubenstein's. Today's Will's birthday, so they're having a party."

"Oh, that's too bad. Rick, we'll find out all the great stuff to do in Chesterfield, and you can come next time."

Ricky seems less than excited by the prospect. "Okay," he says.

"What about Tara and Sebastian?" Laurie says, looking for an out. "They'd be alone a long time. Is this important, Andy?"

"Probably not, but it's a box I have to check. With all that was going on, Benjamin took the time to drive down there; I'd sort of like to know why. If you don't want to come, I understand."

She smiles. "Are you kidding? I wouldn't miss it."

So an hour later, we've dropped Ricky off at Will's house and we're on the road to Chesterfield. Tara and Sebastian are in the back. Tara as always is up and looking out the window, while Sebastian sleeps next to her. It's fair to say that Sebastian does not devour life.

Chesterfield is only about an hour-and-fifteen-minute drive from Paterson. It's mostly the New Jersey Turnpike, and then it's about a twenty-minute drive from that highway to Chesterfield. It's a rainy day, so we don't hit much traffic, since there are not many people heading down to the shore.

I only have three places that Eric Benjamin visited, as determined by where he'd used his credit card. One is a gas station, and we stop there. New Jersey bizarrely still prohibits self-serve gas pumping, so I ask the guy who does the pumping if he recognizes the picture I have of Eric Benjamin.

No surprise; he doesn't. We're making a lot of progress here.

Next, we stop at the hotel where Benjamin stayed. It's a Holiday Inn Express; comfortable enough but not the lap of luxury. Of course, if Benjamin wanted to be in this area, he didn't have many choices. No one will confuse Chesterfield with Vegas.

Once again, we get nowhere; none of the hotel employees we show the photograph to say that they remember.

So off we go again, driving around looking mostly at farmland. There are no signs saying, "Vicious murderer stopped here," so we don't learn much. All in all, it's pretty boring.

"Can we come here again next week?" Laurie asks. "There's just too much to do in one visit."

"I told you I'd show you a good time. Are you hungry?"

"We just had breakfast a couple of hours ago."

"Me too," I say. "Let's go eat."

We head for the restaurant that Benjamin had been to, a diner cleverly named the Chesterfield Diner. Unfortunately, we can't use the outdoor tables because it's starting to rain, and they say we can't bring Tara and Sebastian inside.

"State law," the diner worker says. "You could take them to the Lazy Dog Diner. It's a mile down the road."

"They don't obey the state law?"

He shrugs. "Guess not."

Laurie, Tara, and Sebastian wait in the car while I ask every worker in the diner if they recognize Eric Benjamin. They don't.

On to the lawbreaking Lazy Dog Diner.

It's a fairly small place, with seven tables and a counter. Three of the tables are occupied, and there are four people at the counter. There's a smell I notice, like potpourri or something, probably designed to mask accidents by the patrons.

Each of the three occupied tables has a dog with the people, but there are no dogs with the counter patrons. We take one of the tables, and a waitress immediately comes over with water dishes and dog biscuits.

This is my kind of place.

I am constitutionally incapable of seeing a dog and not petting it. I'm just drawn to them. So while we're waiting for our food, I walk over to each table and ask the people if I can pet their dogs. All of them agree, as I knew they would. Dog owners like to show off their dogs. They're also proud of them, and the fact that a stranger would be drawn to them is a form of confirmation of their greatness.

Of course, these people will never have a dog nearly as great as Tara, but I don't need to throw that in their faces.

I ask each group of people how old their dogs are, how long they've had them, and so on. It's just babble designed to keep me there, petting away.

At the third table, sitting with a young couple, is a mutt of some sort, maybe fifty pounds, but long and lanky. I'm thinking maybe a Lab-hound mix, although it's impossible to tell. People who try to guess the mixture in mutts are spinning their wheels. It's not like two purebreds mated; chances are each of this dog's parents were the products of many different ancestral mixes.

"How old is he?" I ask.

The woman at the table says, "We don't know. The shelter said probably three, but there's no way to tell." She talks to the dog. "And you won't tell us, will you, Boomer?" Then, to me, "The shelter gave him that name, but it felt right, so we kept it."

"Good; you rescued him from a shelter? From around here?"

She laughs. "Not exactly. The shelter is in Little Rock, Arkansas. He came a long way to find us."

"A rescue group brought him up?" I ask.

Now it's the man's turn to talk. "Seems like it. We found him stray with a tag saying he was from this shelter down in Little Rock. So we called them, and they ID'd him. They were damn annoyed that he was running stray."

"When was this?"

"About four months ago. Actually, it was on my birthday, May 14." He stares at his wife. "It was the only present I got."

She laughs. "Sorry, honey."

I ask everyone in the restaurant if they recognize the Eric Benjamin photo and also if they've seen a tractor trailer filled with dogs. I get negative responses all around and some weird looks when I bring up the dog-filled tractor trailer.

I know it's a stretch, but I'm betting that the hound mix was on Kenny Zimmer's truck from an earlier trip than the one that ended in his death; the Little Rock connection cannot be a coincidence. It ran away, maybe while being walked. And Kenny probably made no effort to find it, because Kenny didn't give a damn about dogs.

But what it means is that both Eric Benjamin and Kenny Zimmer were in Chesterfield. I don't know if they were ever there together, and I sure don't know why they were there.

But somehow I've got a feeling that the answer to a lot of questions is in Chesterfield, New Jersey.

The defense calls Dave Kramer."

Kramer stands and walks forward, taking the oath to tell the truth and then sitting in the witness-box. He seems calm and collected, unlike his lawyer, who is rather nervous. I don't like it when my clients testify.

I start off by taking him through the event two years ago when he beat up Kenny Zimmer. "Why did you do it?" I ask.

"He molested a young girl. He admitted it and laughed about it. I would like to say that I did it because I knew that otherwise he would get away with it without being punished. But I wasn't thinking that clearly; I was just so angry at what he had done, and his attitude about it, that I lost control for a moment."

"Did you regret it later?" I ask.

"No."

He talks about how he threatened Kenny that if anything like this happened again he would kill him, and about losing his investigator's license as a result of the incident. I'm getting all of this on the record, because I know that otherwise Carla will do it on cross-examination, and she'll make it sound worse.

"And did you have any contact with Zimmer for the next two and a half years?" I ask.

"None whatsoever."

"Did you think about him? Plan violence against him?"

He smiles slightly. "I did not. He never entered my mind."

"Did you then speak to him at any point?"

"Yes. He called me. Twice actually, to set up a meeting."

"Did he say what the subject of the meeting was to be?"

"He said he had information to help me on a case I was working on. When I asked why he would want to help me, he said it would be good for both of us."

"Did you believe him?" I ask.

"Of course not. If Kenny Zimmer ever told the truth, it would be by accident."

He goes on to say that the meeting was planned for the rest stop, that Zimmer said he would be on his truck. He agreed to meet with Zimmer mostly out of curiosity as to what he could possibly want.

Kramer says that he waited for him to arrive, and when he did, he boarded the truck. All of that is confirmed by the video.

"What happened when you boarded?" I ask.

"At first nothing. I didn't see him; I just saw all these dogs in cages. They were barking like crazy. Then suddenly Zimmer jumped out from behind a pillar and swung this large knife at me . . . at my throat."

"What happened next?"

"He missed me, just by a few inches. Then he came after me again and I avoided it. I took out my gun and I shot him before he could swing at me a third time."

"Could you have run off without shooting him?" I ask.

"Not without taking a big risk. There were dog cages around, so I would have had to turn around to find a direct way out. He could have gotten me from behind with the knife."

Then Kramer says that he left after confirming that Kenny was in fact dead. He describes how he left the note for the police and came to my house, where he was arrested.

After that, I finish up by taking him through his work investigating the Craddock death, and I introduce a police report that his house was broken into, with the files ransacked. He said that there was a Craddock file in there, but the police did not include it in their inventory, so it must have been the target of the theft.

All in all, he comes off as credible and likable, but that was on direct examination. That is the easy part.

Carla approaches the bench. "That was quite a story, Mr. Kramer."

"Thank you," he says, immediately violating my instructions. He was being sarcastic, or at least tongue in cheek, and I cautioned him against it. He's on trial for his future, and under no circumstances is it remotely a joking matter.

"So you were so furious at something Mr. Zimmer said to you that you lost control and assaulted him?"

"He said he molested a child."

"Please answer the question, and I think you can cover it with a yes or no. You were so furious at something Mr. Zimmer said to you that you lost control and assaulted him?"

"Yes."

"And then you threatened his life?"

"If he were to do something like that again," Kramer says.

"And now this terrible person, whose life you threatened and who must certainly hate you for beating him up, calls and wants to have a meeting."

"Yes."

"And you think, *Sure, why not? I'll go see my old buddy, who I haven't seen since I put him in the hospital.* Is that right?"

"Yes."

"Did you think he might attack you?"

"I thought it was possible."

"But you weren't worried?"

"No."

"What if he'd had a gun rather than an invisible knife?"

"I have confidence in myself in situations like that."

"You're comfortable with violence?" she asks.

"I can handle myself when I have to. I spent a lot of years in the service and on the police force learning how. I try not to have to use what I learned."

"Why did you run away?"

"I wouldn't characterize it as running away. I left the scene."

"I didn't ask you to characterize it; please answer the question."

"I left the scene because I was concerned that with my history with Zimmer, the police would not believe that it was self-defense. Unfortunately, I was proven correct."

"You mean the fact that Mr. Zimmer had no weapon while you had a gun wouldn't look like you were in mortal danger?"

"He had a weapon."

"I forgot. The invisible knife."

All in all, Carla goes at him like this for almost an hour. He holds up well, better than I'd expected, but the picture of what happened that day is not a positive for our side.

But it could have been worse. It could always be worse.

Judge Avery asks if I have any other witnesses to call, and I respond by speaking the scariest words in the trial lawyer's vocabulary.

"Your Honor, the defense rests."

Every element of the operation was difficult. Raising seed money. Finding investors. Removing obstacles. Getting the weapons into the country. Finding and building the perfect location. Moving them into position.

Only one real task remained—to wire them in such a way that they could be fired remotely—because Rodgers did not want to be there when the authorities realized their source.

And that would happen quickly.

After that, all that would be left to do would be to take in the money and give the investors their share.

Then the manhunt would begin, and the fingers would be pointed.

But Rodgers would be gone by then.

Because Rodgers didn't exist.

C losing arguments are today, and I'm more anxious than usual. Of course, I'm rarely anxious at all, so it isn't a high anxiety bar to clear. But unless I can somehow reach the jury in a way I haven't so far, I believe we're going to lose.

I spent last night going over the points I want to make. I never write out what I am going to say in detail; I think it hurts the spontaneity. This approach has always worked pretty well for me in the past.

But I'm still a bit edgy, so on the way to court, I stop at the Tara Foundation. Petting the dogs, throwing a tennis ball for them to fetch, things like that tend to relax me. The fact that their lives are so simple, their needs and their joys so obvious and uncomplicated, somehow helps clear my mind.

I arrive at 8:00 A.M., and Willie and Sondra are already here, walking and feeding the dogs. They are remarkable in their dedication, and I truly believe that they are telling the truth when they say there is nothing they would rather do with their time.

I pet them all, but as always, I am drawn to the golden, Wiggy, and her puppies. The puppies have reached the age where they can be placed in homes. Everybody is going to want them, and Willie will be incredibly rigorous in his screening of the potential adopters. Only the best dog homes satisfy Willie.

There are twenty-two dogs left from the original group, including Wiggy and the puppies. I'm still puzzled that Zimmer had no destination set up to receive them, or at least none that I know of.

"They'll all be in homes in a couple of weeks," Willie says. "We've got applicants lined up and waiting. It's been great."

"Maybe we should look into doing this more often," I say. "If you're up for it."

"You mean bringing dogs up from down South? I'll talk to Sondra, but I'm sure she'll want to do it. It's a great idea."

"We'd have to get reliable drivers," I say. "It's a big responsibility. I saw a dog down in Chesterfield that I think got lost from one of Zimmer's runs."

"What kind of dog?" he asks. It's a simple, ordinary question, but it hits me like a ton of bricks.

"Willie, remember you said there was an empty cage on the truck, that a dog was missing?"

"Yeah. Why?"

"Do you still have the card that was on his cage? Did it say what kind of dog it was?"

"Should be in the office; let me check."

He goes off, leaving me with Wiggy to talk to. "Wig, this could be big."

Willie comes back with the card in his hand. "It says he was a hound mix, three years old."

"Does it have a name on it?"

He nods. "Boomer."

It's getting late enough that I need to leave for court, so I call Sam Willis on the way. "Sam, please drop anything else and find out whatever you can about George Davenport. All I have on him is his cell phone number and the fact that he operated the dog transports and owned the truck. And he said he placed ads on Craigslist; that's how he found Zimmer."

I give Sam the number, and he says he was in court the day Davenport testified, so he knows what he looks like. That will somehow help in the process, according to Sam. It's something about Google images . . .

I arrive in court about thirty seconds before Judge Avery takes his seat on the bench.

"Everything okay?" Kramer asks. He's surprised at my timing, since I'm usually there at least fifteen minutes before court is called to order.

"It just might be," I say.

don't like to blow my own horn," Carla says. Then she puts on a fake sheepish smile. "Well, actually I do; I just wish I had more opportunities. But this is one time I was right, and I'm not too modest to say it.

"The very first thing I told you at the beginning of the trial was that this was an important responsibility that you were undertaking, but that did not mean it was going to be difficult or complicated.

"And I was right. It's a straightforward case and has been from the beginning. Mr. Carpenter has tried to muddy the waters, bringing in extraneous crimes and villains, but he hasn't come close to denting the core of this case.

"David Kramer murdered Kenny Zimmer. That's what it has been about from the beginning. It doesn't matter what Eric Benjamin did to John Craddock or whether Victor Andreson slept with a prostitute. That is all designed to confuse you, to make you throw up your hands and say that you can't keep track of all this.

"But he underestimates you; you can and have been keeping track. All you had to do was focus on the issue you are here to decide and let some other future jury worry about the rest.

"David Kramer hated Kenny Zimmer to the point where not only did he beat him up once, but he then threatened his life. So he met Mr. Zimmer in a truck at a deserted rest stop, where no one could be a witness, and he shot and killed him. And then he ran.

"He says it was self-defense, that Mr. Zimmer attacked him with a knife. Well, where is the knife? Mr. Carpenter would have you believe that a third party was on the truck, and he removed the knife. In fact, he said they parked the truck so that the person could leave without being seen by the cameras.

"I submit that makes no sense. Why plan an exit, when the real plan was for Mr. Kramer to be dead? And why did the third person not kill Mr. Kramer when Mr. Zimmer supposedly failed to do so? He could have used a gun, which is a bit more effective and a bit more certain than a knife.

"And through the wonder of security cameras, you saw a great deal of it. And at least as important as what you saw is what you didn't see; the mysterious fleeing third person. And by the way, where did that third person go? Did he carry the invisible knife out to the highway and then hitchhike home?

"No, ladies and gentlemen, this is not a tough call. You saw what he did, you know what he did, and I have no doubt your verdict will reflect it. Thank you for your service."

Carla has done an effective job in getting the jury to consider the main facts, the ones they can see clearly. I have to now switch their focus to that which is not so clear, the outside conspiracy that I have brought in. I'm at a clear disadvantage here.

"Ladies and gentlemen, like Ms. Westrum, I would like to take you back to the start of trial, to what I said in my opening statement. I told you that you would have to rely on logic and common sense, and that remains true.

"But for the moment, and only for the moment, I want you to use your imagination. I've presented witnesses with some hypotheticals during this trial, and I want to give you one too.

"Imagine that you came to court this morning, and Judge Avery said he had something to discuss with you. He told you that there was a police action last night, and arrests were made, and a conspiracy uncovered. And among the things that were learned in the process was the fact that Kenny Zimmer in fact tried to kill David Kramer, and Eric Benjamin in fact did remove the weapon from the truck.

"What do you imagine your reaction would have been? Some surprise that I was right all along? Relief that you would get to go home and not have to listen to lawyers babble anymore? Either of those re-actions would make perfect sense.

"But I'll tell you how I don't think you would have reacted. I don't think you would have said, 'Judge, that's just not possible. You must be mistaken, because what you are saying defies reason.'

"And that is because I have presented a plausible theory. And most importantly, it's a theory backed up by facts. For example, it is a fact that Kenny Zimmer received $75,000 from a mysterious source just before this incident.

"It is probably more money than he had ever had in his life, and why did someone give it to him? I presented a logical reason, that he was being paid to commit a murder. Did Ms. Westrum give you her version of it? If she did, I didn't hear it.

"Eric Benjamin's fingerprint was found on the truck. I gave you my theory as to why it was there. Did Ms. Westrum give you her version of it? If she did, I didn't hear it.

"Eric Benjamin was part of a massive criminal conspiracy. Part of that conspiracy was the murder of John Craddock. David Kramer was investigating that murder and was in a position to expose the con-spiracy.

"So Eric Benjamin conspired to either kill David Kramer or get him arrested. Either outcome was fine, because either outcome would re-move Mr. Kramer and protect the conspiracy.

"Is that so hard to imagine? Doesn't your logic and common sense say it could have happened that way? Is it unreasonable to think it's possible?

"If you utilize the common sense and logic that I told you was nec-essary, you will realize that there is not only a reasonable doubt but a very strong doubt that David Kramer murdered Kenny Zimmer.

"And you will do the only thing you can reasonably do. You will vote to acquit."

Judge Avery gives his charge to the jury and sends them off to de-liberate. I hope they take a long time. If they're going to side with us, then it means they bought into a nuanced argument that will take time to sort through.

If they go with the prosecution, then they're more interested in the nuts and bolts. When Kramer got on that truck, Zimmer was alive. When he got off, Zimmer was dead, and it was Kramer's gun that killed him.

Case closed.

I call Givens at the FBI even before I hear from Sam.

Once again, he comes right to the phone. "I hope you have something for me. I'm getting a little tired of chatting."

"We have something for each other," I say. "We need to meet tomorrow morning at 7:00 A.M."

"I don't get in until eight."

"That's okay. We're not meeting at your office; I'm choosing a neutral site."

"You think a meeting can have home field advantage?" he asks.

"I have my reasons," I say.

I give him the name of a diner in East Rutherford, and he says, "You need to tell me what this is about."

"It's about everything you need to know. I've got it all."

"Why am I not convinced?"

"Let me ask you a question, Givens. Do they have federal school crossing guards? Because if you blow this, that's your next assignment. And you'll have to buy your own whistle."

I hang up before he can respond; I don't want to give anything else away. My next call is to Sam, who starts with, "George Davenport doesn't exist."

"That's what I thought," I say.

"The phone number is in a fake name, and he sure as hell never placed an ad on Craigslist. And Kenny Zimmer never answered it."

"Sam, can you wire me up for a conversation so it can be recorded?"

"Of course."

"How long will it take for you to get the material? I need it by—"

"I've got it. I'll bring a few sizes just to be sure."

"Sam, you're a little weird."

"That's what Hilda says."

I ask Sam to be at my house at 5:30 A.M., and he has no problem with that. In the meantime, I explain everything to Laurie, and she says, "I'll set it up for Ricky to go to Will Rubenstein's after school tomorrow. Marcus and I are going to Chesterfield."

I'm not going to argue with her; what I'm doing is risky, and Laurie and Marcus being down there cuts down on the risk, at least to some degree.

But not nearly enough.

Sam is here at five thirty sharp with enough spy paraphernalia to stock the Moscow branch of the CIA. It takes him forty-five minutes to put it on me; he does it expertly, as if for him it's just another day at the office. He must have an interesting accounting practice.

I'm in the parking lot of the diner at six forty-five. I keep the car running, and when Givens parks and gets out of his car, I pull up to him. "Get in," I say.

"You've been watching too many spy movies," he says.

"You can lecture me when you get in the car."

He shakes his head in annoyance, but gets in. I drive the car around to the back of the parking lot and stop. "We're going to talk here?"

I nod. "Right here."

"You've got five minutes, James Bond."

know where the missiles are and how they're going to be used."

Givens looks at me for a few moments and says, "Then I might be willing to extend the five-minute deadline. How did you know they were missiles?"

"Because of where they are," I say. Then, "Benjamin was responsible for the crash in value of Roboton and Victor's Donuts. He killed Craddock and framed Andreson."

"Is this about your stock manipulation scheme?" Givens asked. "I've got more important things to worry about."

"No, you don't. Because it's all one thing. You think that those missiles you're worried about are going to be used to bring down another company. And maybe a lot of people will die in the process."

"And?"

"And you're wrong."

"How am I wrong?"

"I'll get there. But first I want to talk about Dave Kramer. You know he killed Zimmer in self-defense."

Givens feigns an amused expression. "And how do I know that?"

"Because you've been all over this from day one. You took over the Benjamin investigation, which means you searched Benjamin's house. Then you ran a fingerprint of Zimmer, which must have come from that search."

"So?"

"So it had to be the knife that he used as the weapon."

Givens doesn't say anything, which in itself says everything. So I continue, "You were willing to let my client be convicted of murder."

"We would have gotten him out either way. We don't let people go to jail for crimes they didn't commit. It doesn't work that way."

"He's already lost almost four months of his life."

"A lot of people are going to lose their entire lives if you don't tell me what you know. I'll see to it that Kramer gets out when the time comes."

"The time comes tomorrow," I say. "Now, do I have your word you'll intervene in the trial?"

"I'll do what I can. Can we get on to more important things?"

"Fair enough. The man who you're looking for, the one who has the weapons and is going to use them, is George Davenport."

"Who the hell is George Davenport?" he asks.

"He doesn't exist."

"You're starting to get on my nerves."

"It's not his real name. He's the guy who owned the truck that brought the dogs north, the one Zimmer was killed on. There was a padded area in the middle of the truck; I thought it was padded because it was the area the dogs could play in and not get hurt if the truck swerved. But it was to carry and protect the missiles."

"Why the dogs?" he asks.

"He had the rescue dogs in front and back of the missiles. If the truck was stopped for any reason, the dogs were a perfect cover for what he was doing."

"What is he planning to do?"

"I don't know the targets, but they're going to be in New York and Washington, maybe even Philadelphia. I doubt that the targets are even important; just the attack itself will serve his purpose."

"What's the purpose?" he asks. I certainly have his full attention.

"When 9/11 happened, the stock market dropped fifteen percent in a week and twenty-five percent overall. Davenport, or whoever he is, is going to cause a market crash by firing these missiles at New York and Washington. It will be bigger than 9/11."

Givens starts to ask a question, but I continue, "And he will have bought put options and spread them out among those industries that will take the biggest hit. For instance, defense stocks will go up, so he'll stay away from them. The stocks he'll hit could go down forty percent."

"And with the options spread out, they'll be undetected."

I nod. "It's all going to be dummy corporations and foreign investors. Roboton and Victor's Donuts were done for the purpose of giving Davenport more money to use in this operation. They will make billions."

"Where are the weapons?"

"Chesterfield, New Jersey. Sitting between New York and D.C."

"You have an address?"

"No. But I would look for a large open building, maybe a barn, and maybe recently purchased or built. And with no other buildings or people in the area."

"You're sure of all this?"

"Sure of some of it, confident in the rest. You got anything to lose by sending your agents to Chesterfield? They have somewhere better to go?"

I got as much as I could out of Givens.

I have to trust him, because basically he has the cards. I could not withhold what I knew; the potential disaster that could result from that would be enormous.

The truth is that I have an absolute reason to believe that everything I told Givens was correct, but that doesn't mean I'm right. Quite a bit of it I would put in the category of very educated guess.

Right now, in the moment, I don't know what to do with myself. Laurie and Marcus should be in the Chesterfield area by now; since they've gotten there so early, she and I agreed that the first place to check should be the Holiday Inn Express where Benjamin stayed. Maybe their criminal conspiracy has a company discount.

I'd like to go down there and help them look, but I'm under instructions from Judge Avery to remain close to the courtroom in case of a verdict. I don't think there will be a verdict this quickly; at least I hope there won't. But you never know.

I call Laurie, and she says that they are just arriving at the hotel now. I ask her to keep me posted, and she promises that she will. I also ask whether she thinks I should come down there, and she says I am better off obeying Judge Avery's direction.

Left unsaid is her logical view that if things turn violent, in this case two is better than three. Or at least as good.

So here I am, sitting in the diner parking lot, frozen in place. I finally reach a momentous decision; I'll go in and have breakfast. That way I can stuff my face while I'm worried about Laurie and also worried that the sudden invasion of FBI agents might spook Davenport into firing the missiles.

I order pancakes, bacon, hash browns, and coffee. Just as they arrive, my phone rings. It's Hike, and his message is simple. "There's a verdict."

I wasn't hungry anyway.

I head for the courthouse with a pit in my stomach the size of a side-by-side washer-dryer. The jury deliberated for only eight hours. That's nothing; it takes Laurie nearly that long to decide what toppings to put on her pizza.

My theory was that a quick verdict would be bad for us. I hope my theory was wrong.

Givens obviously has not had the time to intervene with the court, and I can't say I blame him. He's got other things on his plate right now . . . more important things.

I don't know if he will throw the weight of the FBI behind Kramer if he is convicted and goes to appeal. I have the tape of our conversation, but it can be seen as ambiguous. Also, Givens can say he lied about having knowledge of Kramer's innocence in order to get the information about the weapons from me. It would have been a lie for the greater good.

But even if Givens comes through, the result is far from assured. The appeals process can be very unpredictable, and appeals courts don't casually overturn jury verdicts. They are also very slow; if Kramer is convicted, he will spend considerable time in prison, no matter what.

I arrive at court with ten minutes to spare. Hike is at the defense table, and Kramer is being brought in when I am sitting down. The debate in my mind is whether to tell him about the development with Givens.

I decide against it. I don't know that I could explain it adequately enough in the time we have for him to correctly process it. Better to let things play out; if he's convicted, I can bring him up to speed and in the process hopefully cushion the crushing pain he'll be feeling.

"What do you think?" Kramer asks.

"I think we'll know in three minutes."

Kramer has spent enough time with Hike to know not to ask him.

So we just sit here and wait until Judge Avery comes in. He then brings in the jury. Three of them look at the defense table as they walk in, which is a good sign. On the other hand, nine of them don't.

The foreman confirms that they have, in fact, reached a verdict. The bailiff takes it and hands it to Judge Avery, who reads it. Then he hands it back, and the bailiff brings it to the clerk to be read.

Kramer leans over and says to me, "I didn't know it was possible to be this nervous."

Judge Avery directs Kramer to stand and face the jury. Hike and I stand as well. My legs are shaking; my legs always shake before a verdict is rendered. It is impossible for me to imagine a more stressful time, and I'm only the lawyer.

I put my arm on Kramer's shoulder, an awkward gesture because of his height. If they don't read the verdict quickly, I'm going to tear my rotator cuff.

The clerk stares at the verdict, possibly reveling in the knowledge that she is aware of what is about to be said before everyone else. Finally, she begins.

"As it relates to the case of *New Jersey v. David Kramer*, the charge being murder in the first degree for the criminal death of Kenneth Zimmer, we, the jury, find the defendant, David Kramer, not guilty."

I can feel Kramer sag with relief, he sags so far that's he's almost my height. Then he turns and hugs me. He's really not that great a hugger; I don't know what the hell Laurie saw in him.

"Laurie was right; you're the best," he says.

I can feel my cell phone vibrating in my pocket, and I reach for it. "Speak of the devil," I say. "It's Laurie."

"Hello?"

"Andy, we got him. I'll tell you all about it when I get home."

"Did you find out where the weapons are?"

"Yes. I called Givens. Anything new with the trial?"

"You could say that. Hold on; somebody wants to talk to you."

I hand the phone to Kramer and shake hands with Carla, who has come over to congratulate me. She has a gracious smile on her face; I don't know if I'd do the same if the roles were reversed.

"You're as advertised," she says.

G ivens alerted his superiors, who in turn called in the military.

This was not something within the FBI's area of expertise.

Reconnaissance showed that the barn was filled with Russian-made Iskander-M missiles, on their mobile launchers, ready to be aimed and fired. It is likely that they could have just been removed, with no danger to anyone.

However, there was always the possibility that they were programmed to be launched remotely, on a timer. The fact that they were not rolled out of the barn and in position to launch did not mean that programming had not taken place. The odds were strong that there was no remote programming yet, and no timer, but they couldn't take that chance.

Air force bombers were called in, and bombs were dropped on the barn, with the missiles inside. The concussion destroyed everything in the building but did not cause the explosives in the missiles to detonate. However, the massive heat generated ignited the solid fuel, and that did the trick. The resulting explosion was massive.

It would never be revealed to the public, but it was certainly the first time, and hopefully the last, that the United States military ever bombed New Jersey.

To his credit, once the all clear was given, Givens called Andy Carpenter to thank him and to offer his immediate help with the trial. He wasn't aware that a verdict had been reached.

Marcus was amazing, Andy. We got to the hotel, and the desk clerk looked up Davenport; that's the name he used to check in. I showed him my badge, an illegal act but worth it in this case, and he told us the room number."

Laurie has been off the force for years. She managed to keep her badge; this is only the second time I can recall her showing it and pretending to be active on the force.

She continues, "He asked if he should call hotel security, but I told him I brought all the security I needed with me. So we go to the room and knock on the door. I pretend to be there to deliver towels, and he opens it just a crack, with that chain lock still on the door."

"Marcus," I say.

"Right. Chain locks don't work very well with Marcus. He kicked the entire door down, and we were in the room. I had my gun drawn, but Davenport, or whatever his name is, goes at Marcus."

"Smart move," I say.

"Yes. It turns out the guy was special forces, and he goes into one of these martial arts poses, and he kicks Marcus in the head. And Marcus starts to bleed."

"Marcus bleeds? Actual blood?"

She nods. "If I hadn't seen it, I wouldn't have believed it. Anyway, Marcus stayed calm, and the guy kicked again, and Marcus grabbed his leg. He twisted it in a way that legs don't twist; I mean, I've seen some tough things, and I couldn't watch it.

"But Marcus wasn't finished; he pounded on the guy to the point that I thought he was going to kill him. Finally, he stopped, and the guy was sitting on the floor, back against the bed. So I asked him where the weapons were. At first he didn't answer, and I told him that he was never going to get to use them anyway, that they were going to be found, and that Marcus was going to break every bone in his body until he told us.

"The scary thing is I was telling the truth. Marcus had this look in his eyes that scared me; I don't think he likes bleeding very much. So Davenport told us, and I called Givens right from that room. They must have had a lot of agents in the area, because they showed up in less than five minutes."

"Marcus bleeds?" I ask. "Are you sure?"

As always, our post-trial victory party is at Charlie's.

Present are Laurie, Edna, Willie, Sondra, Hike, Sam, the Bubalah Brigade, Ricky and his friend Will, and Dave Kramer. Vince and Pete are also here, because Vince and Pete are always here, and since I'm paying for them anyway, they might as well join the party.

In deference to the brigade, we now hold the victory parties at 6:00 P.M., because they like to be asleep before dark. Also, this way they feel like we're taking advantage of the early bird special.

I hadn't had a chance to talk to Kramer much in the two days since the verdict, so he has some questions. "How did you know it was Davenport?"

"What first tipped me off was that there was a dog missing on the truck, and we discovered that the dog who escaped in the Chesterfield area at least a month before Zimmer's truck carrying him was supposed to be there."

"So?"

"So the dogs were just props; they never changed. They were just used as camouflage to hide the real purpose, which was to transport the missiles."

"I don't understand," he says.

"They weren't bringing new groups of dogs up North to be placed; they were bringing the same dogs each time. That's why rescue groups didn't know what Sondra was talking about when she called them to ask if they had been getting deliveries of dogs from down South."

He smiles. "I bet using rescue dogs like that really pissed you off."

I nod. "You got that right. But it also triggered in my mind other things that Davenport had said. I have this weird ability to remember conversations; I don't remember what I had for breakfast this morning, but I remember things that were said to me years ago.

"In this case, I started to look at things Davenport said in a new light. For example, he had said that Zimmer answered a Craigslist ad to get the job and would always email him lists of where the dogs were going."

"So?"

"So we knew that Zimmer didn't have a computer, an email address, or even a phone. Sam described him as being in the technological Dark Ages. Also, when I asked Davenport if he had ever heard of Chesterfield, New Jersey, he said no. But in the same conversation he said that there would have been no reason for Zimmer to go that far off the highway to stop there."

Kramer nods. "Got it. How did he know it was far off the highway if he never heard of it?"

"Exactly."

"So what is happening to the people who invested in Davenport's conspiracy?" he asks.

"The FBI is rounding up whichever ones they can find. But it's not going to be easy; they covered their tracks very well, and many of them are outside the country. Greg Hepner's been arrested, though, so that's one down."

"Ironic," he says. "Now Hepner's company will crash, and some other companies and people will profit from it."

"It's the way of the world."

"What about Tina Bauer?"

I shrug. "No sign of her, and I doubt there ever will be."

"Laurie was right about you," he says. "You're the best."

I nod. "She worships the ground I walk on."

He laughs. "So she says."

"What are you going to do now?"

"California. A friend of mine is an investigator out there; we're going to go into business together. Hollywood is filled with cheating spouses just itching to be spied on."

And it's a whole continent away from Laurie, is what I think but don't say.

Everybody seems to be having a good time, even Hike. I ask him what's going on with Darlene, and he says, "I'm moving on."

I don't quite know what to say in situations like this, so I just say, "You need to do what you have to do."

"Exactly," he says. "It'll be fine. I never let anything bring me down."

"Hike, I've always said that about you."

"And Hilda's got a granddaughter she thinks will be perfect for me."

"Go for it. The rugelach alone will make it worth it."

Edna comes over to me and asks, "So I guess we'll take a break for a while now? It's never good to overdo this client thing."

"You think one a year is enough?"

She nods. "You know me; I'm the 'roll up your sleeves and get to work' type. But I don't want you to wear yourself down."

Willie tells me that all the dogs from the truck have been placed, with the exception of Wiggy. "She's a keeper," he says. "And Cash loves her."

Just as Laurie and I head for the door, Kramer comes over to us and says to me, "I certainly hate to bring this up, but we've never talked about your fee."

I nod. "Consider it a gift from Laurie. It was important to her."

Laurie smiles, and I put my arm around her. "Let's go home, woman."